Patrick McCabe

Mondo Desperado

PICADOR

First published 1999 by Picador
an imprint of Macmillan Publishers Ltd
25 Eccleston Place, London SW1W 9NF
Basingstoke and Oxford
Associated companies throughout the world
www.macmillan.co.uk

ISBN 0 330 37703 5

1 3 5 7 9 8 6 4 2

A CIP catalogue record for this book is available from
the British Library.

Typeset by SetSystems Ltd, Saffron Walden, Essex
Printed and bound in Great Britain by
Mackays of Chatham plc, Chatham, Kent

Mondo Desperado

OTHER BOOKS BY PATRICK McCABE

FICTION

Music on Clinton Street

Carn

The Butcher Boy

The Dead School

Breakfast on Pluto

PLAYS

Frank Pig Says Hello
(based on *The Butcher Boy*)

CHILDREN'S STORIES

The Adventures of Shay Mouse

* 'There have been quite a few "mondo" films, I understand – including *Mondo Bizarro, Mondo Pazza, Mondo Mod,* etc. To this august lexicon we can now add *Mondo Bollocks!*, surely a much more appropriate title for this "collection"!'

Bernard Henry, *Ardee Observer*

* 'As one of the original "Cavan Freaks of 1966", I can say that Phildy has got it absolutely right – roving packs of big-hairdo teddygirls, distorto surf-guitar rumbles, the lot! It took me right back to the days outside the Lido Grill, with the chicks in their white vinyl skirts, red-leather Beatle boots and Jackie O spex! Fabbo, Phildy! Like, the most – ha ha!'

Davey 'The Breeze' McCoy

* 'Thai Pop! Cantorock! Dope mules! Leopardskin-wearing Amazons! Human transplants gone horribly wrong! Not to be found here, I'm afraid! This book is about as "mondo" as *The Sound of Music*! Hackball is a complete fraud!'

The Essential Guide To Forgotten Cinema

* 'Smut! But then – I'm old fashioned, aren't I? Just because I don't squeal with delight every time a maniac prostitute in a latex swimsuit decides to section some poor unfortunate derelict with a chainsaw!'

Vincent Macklin (Revd.)

* 'What is the value of depicting human beings going about their business with freshly hacked buffalo parts on their heads? Exploitative in the extreme.'

Noel Carr, *Society*

* 'Would have preferred more *Taxi Driver*-type stories. Or Tony Montana! "Do you want to fuck with me? Fuck you! I'll get rid of you fucking cockroaches!" Fantastic!

But nonetheless, it's a very good book and I, for one, will definitely be buying *MONDO DESPERADO 2*.'

Donie Halligan, Newbliss

A Note from the Publisher

When I first received this manuscript from Phildy Hackball, I was at once confused and astounded, but knew instantly that it was inevitable I should have to meet the author. You can imagine my surprise (me being an ingenue of an English publisher who had never been in Ireland before, much less Barntrosna) when he greeted me in a leopardskin swimsuit, smoking a large cigar, repeatedly peppering me with questions regarding the works of Franco Prosperi, Giuliano Carcanetti and 'the other Italians', of none of whom, I was ashamed to admit, I had ever heard. Much of what happened after that is shrouded in a foggy haze, I am afraid, induced by any number of bottles of the finest whiskey and brandies produced by my host. But what I do remember is being privy to some of the most inspiring conversations it has been my privilege to encounter in all my many years as a publisher. 'Wait till I tell you this one!' and 'The best of the whole lot is . . .' are phrases which now come wisping from the vaults of memory as I recapture the image of Phildy astride the television with the waste-paper basket on his head, triumphantly beating his chest as he sings for me, in its entirety, the wonderful ballad 'The Wolfman from Ardee' (not included here), or lighting another Cuban cigar as, behind billowing clouds of smoke, I hear his rich brown voice intone the first sentences of 'My Friend Bruce Lee' or 'The Boils of Thomas Gully'.

Memories I shall treasure always.

That was three years ago. As to how the opinion-makers

and custodians of the sacred literary flame might react to *Mondo Desperado*, one can only speculate. For my own part, there is little doubt but that these stories establish a new high-water mark as far as English literature is concerned. No one, I feel certain, who comes into contact with them can fail to be affected by them, these wondrous journeyings, eclectic voyagings into the interior, which, for the first time, permit us a glimpse – in the company of the peerless Phildy Hackball – into a world which is truly desperate.

Simon Mitchell

Editor

Phildy Hackball: An Appreciation

What can I say about my buddy Phildy? That it comes as no surprise to me he has produced a book which is about to burst the literary world wide open? Because it sure does not! Right from the very first day I met him, I knew! 'Phildy,' I said, 'you're going to do it! One day you'll send a book flying out of that typewriter that'll leave them all standing!' But little did I know it was going to be a 'mondo'! Although I should have, because me and Phildy – why, we spent our lives sneaking into them! Nudies too – you bet! But mostly mondoes! If we'd been caught, we'd have had our arses kicked into our necks, of course! After all, we were only eight or nine! Oh but boys was it worth the risk or what, watching all them old tribesmen beating each other senseless with poles, bulls having their heads hacked off – and, best of all, of course – sex-change operations taking place somewhere in the backstreets of Asia! Powerful! No surprise then when, years later, Phildy turns to me and says: 'Tell me this, Pat! Did you ever think of becoming a woman at all?' Or when, one day in the Bridge Bar, he looked at me and said: 'Listen, amigo! Who is to say there aren't alien life-forms standing right here beside us now at this very minute?'

A lot of people have said to me lately: 'In all seriousness, Pat – what do you think of these stories of Phildy's? Are they based on his own experiences or what?' To that, I would say that the answer is – yes and no. There is no way, for example, that Phildy would have anything to do with the blowing up of student priests, or the filming of young girls in their pelts. He just isn't that type of person. 'No way, baby!' as one of his characters might say! All he is doing is listening to the stories he hears around him and turning them into literature. And what literature!

Not that I'm any expert, mind you! (Phildy says: 'I'm afraid, Pat, you know as much about Chekhov as my arse knows about snipe-shooting!'), but you won't get better than 'The Hands of Dingo Deery' or 'I Ordained The Devil' in my book. You want to know what I think of Phildy? I think he's fantastic! To tell you the truth – and I don't care who hears it! – if he asked me to marry him in the morning, I'd be off down that Asian backstreet like a shot!

Pat Cork
(Friend)
17 Main Street,
Barntrosna

Mondo Desperado

by

Phildy Hackball

Hot Nights at
the Go-Go Lounge

It's hard to figure how in a small town like this a mature woman of twenty-eight years of age could get herself mixed up with a bunch of deadbeat swingers, but that is exactly what happened to Cora Bunyan and I should know because she was my wife. It is now exactly a year since the nightmare began, when my good friend Walter Skelly first voiced his suspicions, taking me by the arm as we left Louie's Bar and Grill on our way back from lunch to the offices of Barntrosna Insurance. 'Larry,' he said, 'look here. I don't want to alarm you but there's something I think you should know ... it's women – Cora. They have needs, you know what I'm saying? You gotta pay them a little attention, that's all.'

When Walter had finished his story, I could just about stand up. I looked at him and barked: 'I can't believe you'd say such a thing! You – of all people, Walter! Why, you oughta be ashamed of yourself!' He tried his best to apologize but I had already turned away for I wanted to hear no more. 'Get your hands off me!' I snapped and I completed my journey back to the office alone.

But all that afternoon, I couldn't get his words out of my mind. By three thirty, I could stand it no longer. I strode out of my office and stood in his doorway clutching a bottle of ink. 'Walter!' I snapped, and just as he raised his head, I shot the contents of it directly into his face. Before he had time to respond, I was already gone. I knew now why Skelly had tried to poison my mind against Cora. Sure I did – because ever since we'd moved to town, he'd had his eye on her like every other man in this two-bit backwater. I swore to myself that if he ever came near her I would kill him stone dead. With a .357 Magnum I'd put a hole in his head big enough to sleep in. 'You hear that, Skelly!' I snarled at the mirror in the restroom.

If only I'd known then one tenth of what I know now, I would have seen that Walter was only trying to help me. That he was doing what any friend would have considered his duty. But I was blind. Blind! I only had eyes for Cora and she knew that. She'd known it all along.

That night, as I left the office, I had a few more words with Walter Skelly. I told him long as I lived I never wanted to see him again. 'You got that, Skelly?' I growled and flipped a thumb and forefinger at the brim of my hat. He started into saying something about Cora but before he got too far I stopped him and told him that if he was figuring on finding another ink bottle heading his way then that was fine by me; and maybe a smack in the mush for good measure.

I didn't know it, of course, but that was the last opportunity I was to have to do anything about the tragic chain of events about to be set in motion. And now, it was already too late.

As I drove home, I turned the events of the day over in my mind. Even the *thought* of what Walter had done was enough to sicken me right to my stomach. Sure, I knew Cora was a pretty gal and that there were guys in Barntrosna who had wanted me dead when I married her. But to stoop that low, to try and poison a guy's mind against his own wife? The more I thought about it, the more I thought: Walter Skelly is a very sick man.

That was what jealousy had done to him, you see – like

'em all! Hell, even the day we got married, they couldn't let up. Grown men crying! Crying because she'd married me – Larry Bunyan. Who would ever have believed it? The sweetest doll the town had ever seen and what does she do – hooks up with Bunyan! Poor old Larry! Who sits behind his desk all day threading paper clips!

But that was where they had got it wrong, you see! Way wrong! No sir, we Bunyans don't spend our lives threading paper clips. We spend it just like Pop Bunyan did, working our fingernails to the quick building up an insurance firm second to none in this country so that a man can take care of gals like Cora Myers the way they oughta be taken care of – jewels, mink coats, you name it! 'Larry,' she said to me that night by the pool out in Sandlefoot, 'I love you! I want to have your children!' If only she'd known the effect those coupla words had! Why, I guess I must have grown about ten feet tall right there and then! I could see old Pop standing in front of me, puffing on his pipe and resting his hand on my shoulder, saying: 'You see, son? You *have* amounted to something, after all! Son – let me say something! Hell, am I proud of you! Proud, my boy!'

You see, Cora, I want you to know the truth. Fact is, me and Pop – we didn't get along so well when I was a kid. I guess you could say I had disappointed him and which was why he used to meet me coming home from school and say: 'Well, son! What dumbfool thing you do in school today, you goddam useless hobo?' All I wanted was one chance to prove myself – that was all I wanted. And that night in Sandlefoot when you said you loved me and wanted to marry me, why, I felt like tossing my hat across the water and shouting: 'How do you like that, Father! Weren't expecting that, were you, you grizzled old windbag! Ha ha ha!'

Just like the rest of them hadn't! And, boy, did they go half-mad! Now that I had something they'd never get their greasy paws on! Because Cora Myers – small-town beauty, swimsuit model – she belonged to Larry Bunyan now!

Or so I thought. Before the words of Walter Skelly started clinging to my skin like black shining beetles. They say a thought can grow in a man's mind until it becomes an obsession; a tiny grain of salt swell and grow until it fills up a room. They're right.

I had my mind made up. I was going to buy the largest bunch of flowers I could lay my hands on, fling the door open and rush into that house, calling: 'Cora! Stop everything! Put the goddam ironing down! We are going out on the town!'

It had seemed like just about the simplest thing in this world.

Quite what happened that night is still not clear to me. All I can say for sure is that somewhere between the Golden Noodle and the shop where I bought the flowers, something unpredictable happened – a kinda shifting of the psychological axis, maybe you could call it. With the result that as I was returning to the sedan, I found myself thinking: 'What if what Walter says is true?' Perhaps if I hadn't been standing directly outside the newsagents the whole thing might never have happened. But I was, staring through its plate-glass window, in fact, at a stack of magazines, some of which had been robbed of their colour through age, others glossily vivid and – I've got to say it – startling in their directness! One of them in particular caught my eye, depicting the heavily made-up figure of a woman holding aloft a cigarette, her head turned towards me as its trailing smoke curled about her slender white neck, like a scarf of softest silk. And, just underneath, almost defiantly stamped in bold black type: LOVE WAS CHEAP; LIFE WAS HIGH!

It was the lopsided grin on her face, I reckon. Somehow it reminded me of a look that Cora had given me during one of our, I got to admit it, now regular rows. Then there was the blonde – a coiffured lynx in pink knee-high boots and matching spangled swimsuit rolling her eyes at a sweating, skirtless drummer shrouded in cigarette smoke. And across her forehead, in dribbling crimson, the words: *Hot Nights at the Go-Go Lounge!*

Suddenly – I took out my handkerchief – it was as if the window display had become fiercely, insanely alive! The wailing sound of out-of-tune guitars and thundering, palpitating percussion somehow seemed to mingle with a primitive, hysterical laughter that filled the entire street! A redhead in a leopardskin bikini and curves in all the right places leered after me as I fell towards Louie's.

As I sat there in the corner banquette I had it all figured out, and for the first time saw the game my so-called 'beloved wife' was playing. A game called 'Larry Bunyan – sucker'! By the time the last shot went down, everything was clear and I could have hugged my buddy Walter Skelly. How could I have been so foolish? I asked myself. Why couldn't I have seen that all he had wanted to do was warn me! How many times had I seen that look on Cora's face? That pouting mouth, the slightly narrowed eyes that somehow you couldn't trust? And had taken it – for love! The Big Kisser! Had taken it to mean 'Yes! I love you, Larry Bunyan! No matter what anyone else thinks, I love every inch of you!' when, all along, every time she put her hand to her breast and spoke in those mock-dramatic tones was: 'I'm fooling you up to the two eyes but you're too blind to see, Bunyan! Bunyan, the poor fool! Why, he doesn't have enough to stick a stamp!'

As the sedan turned into the curving driveway and cruised

towards our neat little white frame house with its wide yard and two palm trees, I had never felt so good in my life! Boy, did I owe Walter a favour! I owed him now and hell I was gonna pay him back first thing tomorrow with a bottle of Louie's best bourbon!

When I had put a certain little matter to bed once and for all, that is.

To bed once and for all!

*

I decided to play it cool, just like nothing had happened. I hung up my coat in the hallway and tossed my hat onto the stand, just like always. Then I called out, 'Cora? You home, honey?' and smiled when I heard her reply: 'Yes, dear. I'm in the kitchen.' Boy, you really had to hand it to women. One minute they're jitterbugging in some basement dive, fooling around with every two-bit dipso and loser musician, next they're coming on like the sweetest little angel you've ever set your peepers on. But Cora – she was something special! Standing there in her cute little rubber gloves and that dandy little gingham apron – why, she was just about the last person on earth you'd ever figure for a hophead or sex freak.

'So – how have you been, honey?' pulling off my tie and freshening up a little in the kitchenette.

'Oh, you know, dear,' she smiled, 'the usual. Went up the town, got things for the dinner. Paid the gas bill. Nothing special.'

No, nothing special, I thought, as I wiped my face with the towel, just a little 'exotic dancing' and a handful of reefers with your sleazeball friends, a little bit of 'twisting' with some dubious photographer and his beatnik pals, sure, why the hell not, go right ahead – get out of your minds! Flap your arms and shake your beehive heads to some crazy trashy instrumental rock! After all – it's nothing special, is it? No, ha ha! Nothing much special ever happens in the Go-Go Lounge, does it? Does it, Cora?

Cora Myers who used to be my wife!

Not that I said it, of course. Not yet! I might be dumb like Pop said but I sure wasn't gonna blow my wad straight away! Oh no. I was gonna let her have all the rope she needed. Besides, I was curious to see just how long she could keep her little charade going.

'So – how are they?' she said with a smile would make dead roses bloom.

'What? How's what?' I said, kind of taken aback by the sudden realization of just how beautiful my wife was – them sparkling blue eyes, blonde hair, finely chiselled features – quite aristocratic – and foolishly almost blowing my cover.

'The chops, of course!' she said, gliding towards the kitchenette and humming to herself as she stacked the crockery on the draining board.

'The chops! Why – they're fine!' I called out. 'Matter of fact – they're just about the damned tastiest chops I've ever had, in this house or anywhere else, Cora!'

'I'm glad!' she said, and continued humming – just a soft, regular tune, just about as far from 'Beat Girl' or 'Bachelor Party Bunny' as it was possible to get and showed you just how clever little Miss Cora Myers could be! It was difficult at that moment not to dump the chops on the floor right where I sat and get it all over with there and then. To cry: 'Why! What has gone wrong! Why all of a sudden are you behaving like this! Maybe it is true! Maybe I don't have enough to stick a stamp but you could have told me! After all we've been through, Cora, you could have told me! You didn't have to go running off – there! Where to after this? *The Harem Keeper of the Oil Sheiks? The Mini Skirt Mob? Nightmare Rampage of the Hellcats?* Cora! You hear me – Cora Myers?'

*

As I sat there I could hear it all plain as day. See myself standing right there in front of her, pulling no punches as I said it loud and clear. But it wasn't the only thing I could see. I could see her too. Miss Cora 'I swear I'm not a man-eater' Myers, with her arms outspread and her innocent eyes, going: 'Larry, I don't know what you're talking about! Have you been drinking, Larry Bunyan? Because I don't understand a word you're saying!'

I figured on those last coupla words snapping me like a dry twig.

'No! Sure you don't!' I'd snap as I smacked my fist down on the table.

'Honey! I don't understand!' she'd say with, sure as hell, that old trembling hand placed against her throat, those same old mock-dramatic tones!

'No – sure you don't! And you don't slip out of this house every day just as soon as you get me gone, either! You don't climb into your figure-hugging pants and hit the club in your dragster to meet your so-called "with-it" friends? Just who in the hell do you think you are, Cora? Mamie Van Doren? Go on then – laugh! Laugh at him, the mutthead of a husband who hasn't the faintest idea what you've been up to! Except that's where you're wrong, baby! Sure, I'm a mutthead, a mutthead who happens to be lucky enough to have a good friend by the name of Walter Skelly who put me on to you just before it was too late. Surprised, huh? Thought you might be! Yeah, your little wheeze has been rumbled, Cora baby!

And now the whole world's gonna know it – and you know why? Because I'm gonna see that they do! This time around, Larry Bunyan's through taking it! I'm gonna show you and I'm gonna show them! Hey! Hello there! I'm Larry Bunyan – I don't have enough to stick a stamp! But what I do have is a little self-respect! You listening to me, drop-out wife?'

It was the greatest feeling in the world thinking it all through for myself that way and as I wiped my mouth with the napkin, I looked right over at her and smiled.

'Cora,' I said, 'I could have eaten that dinner and ten more like it.'

'My, but you're in good humour today, Larry,' she smiled as she removed the plate, 'it's not often you say that to me.'

'I guess it isn't,' I said, 'not that it would make a lotta difference either way for most likely you'd be too hopped out of your head to hear it anyway.' The words were outa my mouth before I knew it – I coulda cheered, goddamit!

'What?' she responded, in, of course – mock-dramatic tones!

'Oh, come now, Cora,' I said, before she got a chance to get into her stride, 'there's no need for all that!'

Her trembling hand stroked her throat as I continued.

'You might be good at making dinners but when it comes to acting – well, you might be good! But you're not *that* good! Not that good at all, babe!'

'What . . .' she began, twisting a corner of her apron, 'what on earth are you talking about?'

I spread my legs on the chair and faced her squarely, stabbing the air uncompromisingly – I had come so far, now I was prepared to go all the way – with my rock-steady forefinger.

'You know what your problem was, baby? You want to

know what you did wrong? You got careless, honey! Started flying so high you thought you were so far up no one could touch you! One too many reefers, I guess! Thought Mutthead wouldn't notice? Well, you were wrong, Cora Myers! Way wrong!'

'Wrong about what?' she said – them blue eyes beginning to fill up now! – still keeping up her Little Miss Lost-in-the-forest act. 'Larry – what is wrong with you? How long were you in Louie's? Larry – for God's sake! What are you *talking about*? What is wrong with you?'

I stood up and ran my hands through my thickly Brylcreemed hair. I sighed and looked down at the toes of my brogues. I couldn't believe it. I just couldn't believe she was going to go through with it to the bitter end.

'Wrong?' I said, as I yanked her to me. 'I'll tell you what's wrong! Wrong is two little babies sleeping upstairs while their mother sneaks out to some godforsaken sleazehole to feed her habit; wrong is popping Quaaludes and shovelling gin like it's going out of fashion! Wrong is clinging silk and red lips pouted for kissing! Sax players and brown bosoms throbbing with love! Wrong? I'll tell you what's wrong! Not giving a damn about the things that keep you straight in this world – the things you're supposed to care about! That's what wrong is – two babies with a mother who's a hopped-up swimsuit model in some squalid pit of sexual depravity!'

There were tears in her eyes now, so many she could have washed the floor with them right there and then.

'But Larry!' she cried, she implored, fixing me with them big blue eyes – the old turn-him-to-mush trick! 'We don't have any kids! We can't have – because of . . . you know why, Larry!'

14

She broke off and turned away, thrusting her knuckles into her mouth. I flung the chair aside and spun her around.

'Go on then, say it!' I challenged her. 'Why? Because I don't have enough to stick a stamp! Ain't that right, Cora?'

'No!' she brazenly lied, 'it's not true, Larry!'

'Not true, huh?' I laughed, for what else could I do now that it was all out in the open and I saw what had been behind that beautiful mask all along? Strange thing was, I felt like a million dollars.

'So – tell us, Cora! What are they like? These guys you've been hanging out with? These drummer friends of yours, huh? These – ha! – horn players!'

'Horn players? Drummers? What are you talking about? Oh God! Oh God!'

'I gotta hand it to you, Cora! You sure had me fooled! Hell, only for Walter you probably still would have! But now, well, I guess it doesn't matter any more!'

I lit a cigarette and looked at her through the winding smoke.

'I'm leaving you, Cora! And I'm taking the kids with me! I'm sorry, Cora – but it's goodbye!'

Well, boy was I hot – flushed and out of sorts when I'd said my little piece, so I guess you can imagine how I felt when my little honey pie began to laugh. What could I do but shake my head? I just stood there and stared at her as she laughed her pretty little head right off, thinking to myself just how crazy, when you get down to it, this old world really is.

'Larry,' she cried, throwing her arms around my neck, 'you're joking, of course! That's what you're doing, isn't it? The whole thing is a silly joke! And there I was – taking it all so seriously! Phew!'

15

Funny thing is, in a strange kinda way I wish it had been like that. To have been able to say to her: 'Of course I'm joking, Cora, hon! Joking because you are the sweetest creature a guy has ever had the good fortune to hold in his arms – chiselled features, blonde hair and blue eyes, curves in all the right places. Hell – what more could a man want?'

Yep, Cora Myers was a beautiful woman all right – sweetest doll you ever set your eyes on.

But for every silver fox, lounge lizard and lowdown jazz rat in town, not Larry Bunyan.

*

The dumbest thing of all was, when I told Walter the whole story he starts going all kinda funny – like he doesn't know what I'm talking about or something! But then, I guess that's old Walter, ain't it – he's just that kinda guy. Even down to saying he's never *heard* of any place called the Go-Go Lounge!

I guess he reckons now it's all over it's just time to forget – just like with the ink that day it all started.

And sometimes when I see him smile – when I'm passing him a file maybe, or asking for a paper clip – I can read his thoughts just about as loud and clear as if they were my own: 'There he is – my buddy Larry Bunyan! The man who wouldn't take it any more!'

Or when we're sitting in Louie's maybe, his eyes twinkling as he chews on what's left of his waffles, looking over at me with a broad smile that sends out a simple message: 'They said he hadn't enough to stick a stamp – they were *wrong*!'

Like he does every day when we leave on the dot of one thirty, crossing the square as I put my arm around his shoulders and give him the lowdown on Cora the day she realized once and for all that I was on to her. My own best buddy – the guy I have to thank for everything! – staring at me with big wide eyes – almost as big as my ex-wife's, I swear! – as he hoarsely repeats (you wanna hear him!): 'Hee hee! Sure she did! Sure, Larry, old pal! Oh but yes! Of course!' climbing the stairs to our office where our names inscribed in regal gold wait to greet us, through the open window then his giddy laughter pouring out into the square whilst I – to all intents and purposes a bachelor now, of course! – uncork the bourbon and, carefree as any goddam bird, pace the office floor and begin my story anew, Walter's eyebrows leaping as he rubs his hands and chuckles, helpless tears like small rivers coming rolling down his pink and flaking cheeks.

The Bursted Priest

Of all the boys in Barntrosna, Declan Coyningham was definitely the holiest. This was why all the other boys picked on him, of course. Because they were jealous. They couldn't bear to see him walk to church every morning with his missal and rosary beads tucked under his arm. They hated it, in fact, and were often to be heard saying to each other: 'I wouldn't mind ripping that missal to bits. I wonder how our friend Mr Coyningham would like that!' Declan knew they were saying bad things about him. But he forgave them. Forgave them, and did so because he knew in his heart of hearts that they didn't mean it. He often wondered if they had been born somewhere else would they have become prime ministers or rocket scientists. He felt they would. Sadly, however, they weren't born somewhere else – they were born in the Back Terrace, Barntrosna, and once that happened, your chances of becoming prime minister were slim indeed. And no one knew it better than them. Which only resulted in a deepening of their hatred for Declan. They could not accept that just because he was born in a big house with a garden, he could go around the town thinking he was 'all the big fellow', as Toots Agnew sourly put it. Toots, however, had misinterpreted Declan's demeanour. Which found its genesis not in any notion of superiority, but in a desire to do good by his fellow townspeople; *particularly* those who lived in the Backs.

Late at night – when he was a boy – he would often lie

awake in bed, dreaming of that glorious day when he would return to the town as a fully-fledged clergyman; cruise proudly through the bannered streets in an open-topped bus on the side of which bright painted colours ecstatically enthused WELCOME HOME FR DECLAN!, tears of joy filling his eyes as he recognized each face from his childhood, his heart swelling with pride as he saw his old classmates waving and crying triumphantly: 'Hooray for our pal Declan! For this day he has made Barntrosna a happy place!' He would ponder, too, on his mother, who for many long days and nights had selflessly toiled at her knitting machine, waiting patiently for this day which, many times, she must surely have thought would never arrive. And now it had! How many times had he swooned as he thought of her radiant in her green coat and hat, giving him a little wave from the front pew as he knelt down before the Monsignor who was to perform the ceremony. The Monsignor who would be a good friend to Declan throughout his seven long years in Maynooth College. And who, when they had both finished their spiritual reading, would play football with him up against the gable end of the college, or perhaps accompany him to the games room for a spot of well-earned table tennis.

Declan would smile as he thought of those days which, of course, were yet to come. He saw himself scoring a goal and the Monsignor going mad! So furious Declan thought he was going to hit him! 'It hit the post!' he could hear the older man of the cloth shouting, when it was plain for all to see that it simply had not! But in the end, they would, he knew, settle with penalties and all would be well again. Then it would be off with them around the walk ('This gravelled circle of contemplation,' his colleague called it) to discuss the latest gossip in *The Catholic Times* or the Monsignor's forthcoming article in *Far East*.

They say that in the seminary you form friendships which endure for life. That between men, a bond of affection can develop which becomes indissoluble. Of two men, this was most certainly destined to be true – Declan Coyningham and Monsignor Pacelli Harskins.

Testimony to this would be the fact that for years afterwards Fr Declan would descend the stairs – or he would if things were not, tragically, to prove otherwise – to find awaiting him on the front door mat a familiar sight – a small white rectangle of paper – and, secreted inside it, familiar words which no matter how often he read them would never cease to gladden his heart: 'Harskins here! How's tricks?' And there Fr Declan would stand – years into the future – with the letter in his hand, almost as if in another world, catching up on all the latest *sca* (which was to be their own private pet name for scandal) in Maynooth, whilst Mrs O'Sull (as she would affectionately be known – her name in its entirety being O'Sullivan) tugged repeatedly at his elbow. Rubbing his hands and smiling away then as he seated himself at the table, then excitedly exclaiming with a twinkle in his eye, 'Ready for action when you are, Mrs O'Sull!' and launching himself into a fierce attack on his sizzling plate of rashers and eggs.

Which would, of course, please his housekeeper no end. Because she would know Declan in his youth had been a very weak boy. Had, in particular, a tendency towards colds, the reason his mother knitted him a grey balaclava with matching tasseled woollen scarf, and which she had persuaded his teacher Master Petey to allow him wear for the duration of the school day. Initially, the master – perhaps understandably –

had displayed some reluctance. 'As a rule, Mrs Coyningham, you see,' he said, 'the boys are not permitted to wear headgear of any kind in the classroom. It wouldn't be, generally speaking, school policy.' In the end, however, as he knew the family well, particularly old Jack Coyningham, who had been a well-known character and raconteur about the local pubs before he was killed in a buckrake accident (having been perforated), he agreed to make an exception in this instance.

So it is self-evident that Declan was not a strong boy; and also irrefutable that he had a tendency to pick up colds of an often quite distressing severity. But whether or not exercising what might be termed 'the balaclava option' was ultimately a wise course of action, considering what later transpired, must remain for ever open to conjecture.

For it was around this time that Declan's air of 'apartness', that preoccupied sense of purpose mingled with sanctity that seems the lot of those destined for the religious life, began to manifest itself quite clearly. The manner in which he now carried himself, each step carefully measured with almost obsessive exactitude, as if engaged in some private and intensely personal march for Jesus, and, beneath his balaclava, his eyes transfixed by a miraculous image located, it appeared, somewhere directly in front of him. It was as if from him there seemed to shine, as if in some other-worldly Weetabix advertisement, a light of breathtaking clarity. A light that triumphantly declared: 'I am Declan Coyningham. That is my name. And it is my duty to become a priest and save souls in my home town of Barntrosna.'

An assertion which was undeniable; the evidence was there, all around if you cared to look for it – manifested in the softness of his hands; the supple leather of the shoes lovingly

24

polished by his mother every morning; the little miraculous medal pinned to the white cotton of his vest.

The inevitability of Declan's devoting his life to the service of Christ was accepted at a very early stage by the people of the town. Who, in the main, were quite proud that this was the case. After all, there hadn't been a priest ordained in Barntrosna for over ten years, ever since Fr Sean Chisleworth of Turbot Avenue and that seemed like generations ago now. 'We could be doing with another priest,' the parishioners would often remark, 'and sure wouldn't it be great for Mrs Coyningham? I think she has her heart set on it, God love her.'

Which was indeed true. Ever since Jack (RIP) and herself had done *pooley* (which had been their private name for the love act), she had known Declan was destined to take holy orders. If you had asked her: 'But how – can you explain to us, Mrs Coyningham? – how could you possibly have known that? At such an early stage, I mean?' she wouldn't have been able to tell you. Not in concise, empirical language, at any rate. She would just feel her stomach and give you that look, that queer look that seemed to say: 'I can't rightly say. I just knew, that's all.'

When Declan made his first communion, she thought she was going to have to be carried out, collapsing from what she could only think of as a surfeit of almost unbearable pride. 'Oh, if only Jack was here now,' she sniffled into a Kleenex tissue provided by her sister Winnie (Mrs Alfie Baird of Main Street), adding: 'He'd be the proudest man in the town, God rest his soul!'

'Maybe he's watching from heaven,' soothed Winnie, trying not to think of the remains of what had once been her brother-in-law (for it was her who had come upon what seemed a discarded haybag beneath the buckrake on that fateful day). 'Maybe he is,' sniffled Mrs Coyningham as her son Declan appeared out of nowhere, like an angel dropped from heaven, in his beautifully pressed new suit and carrying the polished, zippered missal with its glittering binding of gold which had been a present from his Aunty Gertie. 'My holy boy!' cried both women at once and descended upon him in a flurry of rattling pearls and spontaneously levitating clouds of powder.

Perhaps if Mrs Coyningham had not insisted quite so forcefully on his daily wearing of the balaclava and knitted scarf, events might have taken a slightly different turn. And Fr Declan might still be happily ministering away in the town of Barntrosna, instead of his soul being an infinitesimal speck circling the cosmos, pitifully crying out for someone to direct it homeward.

At religious retreats down the years, a story that has been related with great frequency concerns an artist commissioned by the Church authorities to paint both the image of transcendent goodness and beauty and that of the most unimaginable wickedness. And who, having had the former delivered to him – the luminous, unblemished visage of a young boy – duly completed his task and set off upon his journey to locate its obverse, a badness so foul and repellent no words could ever begin to adequately describe it. Thirty years he spent upon his quest, only to discover that the black-socketed, wild-haired creature he had chosen as the most authentic representation of evil proved to be none other than that very selfsame young boy he had painted all those years before, now corrupted beyond belief, by this egregious world and all its myriad depravities.

The despair of the crushed painter knew no bounds. As did

that of the people of Barntrosna, who now found themselves encountering what had once been Declan Coyningham. What words could they even begin to utter as they gazed upon his hideous figure, for all the world an animated scarecrow as it flailed about the streets on splayed legs with a bottle of methylated spirits held aloft, scornfully gloating: 'Thomas Aquinas! The two ends of a dog's bollocks!' and 'I'll give you informed conscience, you gimpy-looking hoor and that fucker along with you! You hear me?'

*

'NO!' cried the real Declan Coyningham as he shot up now in his bed, beads of perspiration the size of table tennis balls pinging off the wall opposite. For it had – God be praised! – all been but a dream! Declan sighed with immense relief and flung himself upon his knees in thanksgiving. But his relief was premature. For much worse was yet to come – and in reality.

Who can say for certain that things would have been otherwise if the balaclava had not been donned that first day? That Mrs Coyningham would not still be by her post at the knitting machine, instead of eating flies in St Jude's Nursing Home, insisting that she is pregnant with a little girl who is going to be a nun? Who can honestly declare with anything approaching unfailing conviction, 'Look! If Mrs Coyningham had left things the way they were and never minded about the bloody old balaclava, Fr Declan would be above in the chapel saying Mass this Sunday just like he always did!' – none who identified their place of residence as the town of Barntrosna, that much can be safely regarded as far beyond doubt.

What is also beyond doubt is that the events which led to the tragedy which was to befall Declan Coyningham, aspirant clergyman, could be said to have begun not long after eleven o'clock play in Barntrosna Primary School in the year 1964, for that was the day the boys from the Back Terrace decided once and for all that they had had enough of Declan Coyningham and he would have, without further equivocation, to be blown up.

*

What exactly it was that transpired on that fateful day, no one can say for certain; suffice to say that when the news reached Mrs Bobie Coyningham, she completely broke down on the spot, and was never to be quite the same again. Not, however, that she found herself alone in her trauma – for the town in its entirety was destined soon to be in deep shock. After all, it must be remembered that, in those days, Barntrosna was a quiet, peace-loving community. How could it possibly be expected to cope with a tragedy of such appalling magnitude? Certainly, there had been unsettling incidents, particularly during the 'troubled times', such as the night the Black and Tan lorries rolled into town under cover of darkness, raided Bartle Foody's bar and grocery and beat the proprietor to a pulp with golf sticks and, of course, the occasion on which Teresa Carstairs (Mrs) embezzled the entire funds of the Barntrosna Lacemaking Association and decamped to Honduras without ever being heard of again.

But all this was as nothing to what happened to Declan Coyningham who, on that dread day, had only two things on his mind and they were how to surprise his mother with a little treat and how best he might serve the Blessed Virgin Mary the mother of God, now that the month of May (her special time) was upon us. Which was why it took him completely by surprise when 'Fish-hook' Halloran, Nailie Hopkins and one or two others emerged from their hiding place behind a wall and barked: 'Hold it! Stop right there, Coyningham!'

Initially, Declan was quite pleased, but his good humour and sense of bonhomie began to dramatically evaporate when Fish-hook pulled the tassel of his woollen scarf in a clearly aggressive manner and snapped: 'Look here! This has gone far enough, Coyningham!' With the conversation taking this turn, Declan became somewhat alarmed. Which he was indeed correct in doing, especially now that Fish-hook was glaring at him like a man possessed, with the fleshy tip of his tongue darting in and out like a serpent's. There was only one thing Declan could think to do and that was to say the prayer his mother had taught him, the little prayer to St Anthony for intercession in times of great distress. A definition which most definitely applied now, Declan realized, as Fish-hook gruffly wrenched the missal from his hand and demanded: 'What's this? Prayers, eh? Pshaw!' flinging it disdainfully across the hedge. Declan emitted a shriek of horror and cried out. He explained that it had been a gift from his Aunty Gertie but Fish-hook disdained his pleas with a wide sweep of his mucus-silvered arm, explaining that he didn't care who gave it to him, all that mattered now was that Declan's carry-on had to end once and for all. Because he was somewhat uncertain as to what exactly Fish-hook was talking about, Declan ventured tremulously: 'What carry-on is that, F-F-Fish-hook?'

Which was unwise in the circumstances because it only succeeded in further deepening the rage of his glowering adversary. 'What sort of carry-on?' he snapped. 'Don't play dumb with me, Coyningham! You and your stupid balaclavas, that's what! We've about had it with you! Acting the big fellow! Ha! Look at the big fellow now, lads!' to which his predatory companions responded with a guttural 'Haw!'

When Declan tried to explain that it had never been his intention to act 'the big fellow', the response was nothing more than a bewildered shaking of heads. 'Oh no,' Fish-hook said, 'of course it wasn't! And I suppose the next thing you'll be trying to tell us is that you don't deserve to be blown up!' At this, raucous laughter erupted ecstatically skyward as small tears came into Declan's eyes. 'There's one thing I'll say for you, Coyningham,' continued Fish-hook wearily as he took him by the arm, 'there's no doubt about it! You've definitely got some neck!' Declan meekly permitted himself to be led away as in the distance – although his captors were but a few feet away – he heard: 'Come on, lads! Let's get this over with! We haven't got all day!' to which his eager minions responded eagerly: 'Yep, Fish-hook! Whatever you say, Fish-hook, sir!'

In a way, there was a strange beauty about being led away to be blown up, Declan reflected, as they passed the railway gates, going towards McConkey's field. An odd sense of comfort, of journey's end, in that he intimately knew the place in which he was to meet his demise, and had done for most of his admittedly brief time upon this earth. A privilege which, he was well aware, had been denied to the Saviour in His particular time of trial, never having seen Calvary before in his life. So it was that when he heard Fish-hook cry: 'OK, lads! Off with the trousers, then!' the sound of angels singing behind McClarkey's Garage came as no surprise to him. And why he felt no pain, only resignation, as Fish-hook deftly inserted the nozzle of the air hose snugly between his sad but acceptant buttocks. Why, there was not the slightest trace of vindictiveness or thought of revenge when he heard Fish-hook trumpet: 'Right, boys! Start pumping! Pump! Pump away there like the clappers!' as gleefully, they complied.

Quite how long the eccentric execution took it is impossible to estimate with any degree of accuracy. Suffice it to say that within mere minutes Declan, who had up until then been of average, unremarkable schoolboy size, had become a truly hideous, bladderesque monstrosity, with, paradoxically, upon his face an expression of almost total peace, if not ecstasy, which persisted right up until the very last moment before he finally did, in fact, rend asunder.

It seems superfluous to state that the days which followed were sad. Perhaps if Declan had been knifed, or shot, or even blown up in what might be considered the normal way, the good folk of Barntrosna might have found some means of assuaging their grief. . .who can say? One thing is for certain – the task of gathering up various pieces of the now-decimated schoolboy, which fell to Skinner Moran, had an undeniable effect on him for the rest of his mortal days. It was not unknown for him to begin laughing whilst strolling up the street, seemingly for no reason whatsoever. In the end too, Declan's Aunt Gertie had to be taken away and this gave rise to much local sadness. Particularly when, on being assisted into the ambulance, she insisted on smacking the attendant playfully on the shoulder, tittering: 'Arra, leave me alone! I can manage perfectly well myself!' as she paused then to add, with a glazed and unsettling, wide-eyed look, 'But of all places to find his right eyeball – on the footpath outside the New Pin Cleaners! I ask you!'

Declan's assailants, of course, were packed off to Borstal, only to return some few short months later, infused with a new energy, and are once more to be seen strutting, with renewed vigour, about the town and glaring brazenly at the cowed citizens. 'Just try it,' their malevolent gaze seems to say, 'and let's see what will happen – particularly in the vicinity of McConkey's field!'

But no one has any intention of trying anything, for the qualities of inner strength required for such fortitude are now but a memory; indicating, perhaps, the deepest and most depressingly enduring legacy of Declan's demise – the sense of hopelessness which came to hold the town in a fierce, unyielding grip. Indulgence in all moral thinking now began to appear futile. For, the townspeople found themselves reasoning, how can a deity be possibly said to exist if the wanton destruction of a boy like Declan Coyningham can be so casually countenanced? A boy who lived only for others, who would one day (or so he thought – another cruel, cosmic joke!) have administered the sacraments to all his neighbours, become lifelong friends with Monsignor Pacelli Harskins (in a real, flesh-and-blood relationship far beyond the realm of subconscious longings and dreams on a hot summer night), strolled about the leafy lanes chatting to passers-by and cracking jokes with their growing children, singing lighthearted tunes to dandelions. But who was now nothing more than an awkward assemblage of bones and irregular innards lying in a cold casket in a poorly maintained cemetery.

*

No, dear friends, the truth is that Declan Coyningham was never in fact ordained and now never will be; never live for his mother to see a shining force field vibrate about her son. For her, it has proved but a chimera. As it has for all of us. And now that he lies, along with Aunty Gertie's missal, inert beneath the grass and randomly scattered sweet papers, we know in our hearts that he will never live to see the day when, before cheering crowds, he cruises homeward in that open-topped bus through streets bedecked with bunting.

No, there shall be no evening walks in the seminary

grounds, no private crises of conscience along the 'gravelled circle of contemplation' as small birds twitter in the evenings. For these, like so many of my thoughts about him, now are but as wisps of cloud drifting across the skies of what might have been.

Yes, he is far away now, that pale smiling boy whose soft hands once clasped his zippered missal of calf leather and whose precious words through smiling lips did promise 'Someday I will save the world!', a sentiment which like the thinnest wisp of cloud slowly now makes its way silently above the rooftops, looking down upon me where I stand, moist-eyed, outside the New Pin Cleaners, part of me lost for ever in a world that used to be, before Fish-hook Halloran, fate and the insouciance of an 'all-seeing deity' took the balloon of hope and, mockingly, holding it aloft, repeatedly squeezed until we watched it, like a boy called Declan Coyningham one sad, seemingly innocent day one spring long ago, go 'pop!' before our very eyes.

My Friend Bruce Lee

Incredible as it may seem, the reputation of Bruce Lee as the supreme exponent of exhilarating, sweep-kicking kineticism is not yet secure, and it is indeed far from uncommon to overhear comments so mind-numbingly ill-informed as to be almost stupefying. Comments such as: 'This Bruce Lee fellow! What do you think of him? Is he all he's cracked up to be, do you think? To kung fu what Elvis was to rock and roll or a chopsocky fraud in a warm-up suit?'

It is galling to have to acknowledge that this is the pitiful standard of commentary currently prevailing. And to have to further admit that these would-be – and arrogant, with it! – commentators are not content to leave it at that, but will insist on you accompanying them to a coffee shop or hotel bar where they can proceed with their sententious pronouncements – with your presumed approbation, of course! – not to mention heaping unnecessary derision on the shoulders of a man who, for almost the entire duration of the 1970s, was the undisputed king of kick-boxing. And who, if he were alive today, would soon show these bumptious detractors – who persist in puff-chestedly proclaiming from the rooftops that he is not all he is 'cracked up' to be – just what the word *cracked* really means! It would be straight over a banqueting table in a somersault and a fresh-fish-slapping-on-concrete kick in the jaw for them! But I suppose we ought not be too severe, for, in the end, what can one do but feel pity for them?

For the midgets, that is. For what else are they? If Bruce

...ere alive today, it would take one glare – just one – from his intense, angular face, perhaps accompanied by a gym-towel smack of his hand in the solar plexus, to dispose of a gratifying proportion of their intellectually diminutive number. And if that were to happen, I, for one, would have absolutely no compunction about cheering on the air-slicing killing machine from Hong Kong. 'Who's the sick man of Asia now!' I would cry, as he dispatched them like dominoes right across the floor of the mah-jong parlour.

A deafening silence is what we could expect to look forward to after that particular encounter.

Ever since I completed my book *Bruce Lee and Me*, many people have come up to me and said: 'Tell us, Helmet-Head' – their nickname for me! – 'which of all the Big Boss's films that you have seen would you consider to be your favourite?' It is a question I hear time and again and yet, to this day, I have to confess that it is a teaser that often comes very close to stumping me.

What I found quite extraordinary about the man when I first encountered him was that he was quite unlike himself. By which I mean that if you were anticipating an angry-looking oriental figure, quite small, with two parallel scratches on his cheek and a sleek, short-cut hairstyle – itself not un-like a helmet! – then it is likely you would find yourself very taken aback indeed! I had been half-expecting that, completely without warning, I should find him pantherlike leaping into action – instinctively succumbing to his natural, defensive impulses – catching me around the neck with his legs whilst swinging from the top of a doorframe, or aiming a low-flying kick at my midsection. But, as it transpired, this was entirely misguided, with him being so relaxed in fact that I had to actually plead with him to raise his right leg for the purposes of a photograph. Something else which surprised me also was his manner of speech. Avid viewers of his films will be aware that the movement of the fighter's lips will not always correspond to the sound which is to be heard on the soundtrack, for which reason I felt for a long time that my hero suffered from a slight speech impediment, perhaps the result of repeated asthma attacks when he was a child. Which then led me to wonder was his condition directly related to his being from an early age an eccentrically fluid and masterful kung fu expert? I could only imagine what it must have been like in the school playgrounds of Hong Kong with boys who had been born in the alleys and side-streets of a city plagued with crime going: 'Ha ha! Big chopsocky king! Bruce Lee has asthma – haven't you, Bruce? Go on, Lee – let's hear it! Do your stupid cough for us! *A-haugh! A haugh!* Ha ha – did you ever hear the like of it, boys? Ha hatcha!'

I had fully intended to explore this hypothesis with him, and any other attendant childhood experiences which had a bearing on his becoming such a single-minded and practically invincible one-man crime-busting machine. But, as I alluded earlier, when it turned out he could speak perfectly good English such a need evaporated instantly.

Which came as a welcome relief to me, to be perfectly honest, for one thing I cannot bear is the thought of anyone being teased because of their asthma. It is a most reprehensible practice and I ought to know, quite frankly, for every day after school my own classmates amused themselves by waiting for me on the bridge, hitting me and prodding me relentlessly until I acquiesced and performed a similar ritual for them, which they had quaintly termed 'Helmet-Head Shiteing Razor Blades'. I can still hear their voices ringing in my ears as they mimicked what they insisted was my idiosyncratic manner of perambulation and insisted that I now illustrate it for them, raucously crying: 'That's it, Helmet! Shite some more razor blades for us there! Good man, Helmet-Head McGeough!' pursuing me with a variety of twigs and sticks up and down the length and breadth of the bridge. It is fortunate for them, be assured, that I happened to be in no way endowed with martial arts or kung fu skills, for had I been one thing is certain – I would have demonstrated none of the self-control for which the subject of this little memoir is famous. Within seconds my cry of *'Aiyahhhh!'* would have rent the air and I would have gone through my adversaries like a knife through butter until each and every one of them was laid out on the bridge, folded like a wet noodle. I wonder how many 'Razor Blade' exhortations we'd have been hearing then! Very few, may I be so bold as to venture!

Another aspect of Bruce, which also took me by surprise, was just how friendly and companionable he could actually be! You hear all sorts of stories concerning oriental warriors, don't you? How you are never supposed to know what they are thinking and how, no matter how long you are in their company, be it fifty or a hundred years, you will never be considered a friend by them. Well, I am sorry but I am afraid that in the case of Bruce Lee and myself, nothing could have been further from the truth! For of all the friends I have had in the course of my life, now as I approach my forty-fifth year none of them has meant so much to me as the undisputed king of martial arts. Of course there are those who, to this day, will insist that the person I interviewed and of whose life I have now extensively written was not Bruce Lee at all but someone they had clearly attired to resemble him. A waiter (they claimed!) in the Red Lotus Temple restaurant in Mullingar!

This, of course, is the sort of envious drivel one hears daily in the Bridge Bar from the mouths of those who have nothing better to do than invent rambling incoherent stories to brighten up their otherwise unbearably dreary, benefit-collecting lives. There was a time, I admit, when these people would have mildly irritated me. I am not about to deny that. As neither am I about to deny that if I had been – as I adverted to earlier – fortunate enough to be even mildly proficient in the art of martial polefighting, I would have taken the greatest pleasure in utilizing crossbows, noose contraptions, dangling nets and sharpened plumbing pipes in order to hurl them over the parapets of the bridge and into the roaring waters below.

But, as it has been ordained that this is not to be my lot, I think there can be no better weapon to have at one's disposal than a contempt which is complete and utter. In the early days, when they would call from the street corner, 'Oi! Helmet-Head! Still at the writing, are you? Good man yourself! Ha! Hatcha!' or 'One chicken curry and a pancake roll, please, Helmet!' I would long for the moment when an opportunity to bring the fist of fury to bear on the situation would present itself. But now their taunts I barely hear. I am usually too busy making my way to our local video shop to rent either *Enter the Dragon* or *King Boxer* yet again, to be honest with you! I suppose I ought not to be so surprised when young Martin, the eager assistant, shrugs his shoulders yet again and sighs wearily as he mournfully exclaims: 'Oh no! It's you again! Bruce Lee's best mate!'

By saying which he is overstating it ever so slightly, of course, for I never was, and have never attempted to give the impression that I was, at any time, 'Bruce Lee's *best* mate'. That I might eventually have become such if he had not expired so tragically must remain permanently open to question. Personally, I like to think that I would. But until his untimely death, the truth is that he and I were friends, no more – pen friends, in fact, essentially, apart from the rare occasions when he would pay me a short visit, if he happened to be in the country on business.

To be perfectly frank, the first time I received a letter, I could scarcely believe it! I had not the faintest idea that his personal fan club – to whose advertisement I had responded through the pages of the *Barntrosna Standard* – forwarded the mail directly to him! And was quite taken aback, when I saw before my eyes, the words: 'I would like to come to your house' – in absolutely perfect English! To this day I am astonished that it didn't prompt an instantaneous return of my asthma. No more than the underhand taunts of the Bridge Bar Social Security Association who, that very evening, proceeded to chuckle when they observed me purchasing my lemon soda as I began to consider the astonishing turn of the day's events. Sidling closer to me, if you don't mind, enquiring obliquely as to whether I had purchased the latest *Standard* or not and how much it might cost, did I think, to 'post a letter to China'? I declined to respond, for by then I had become totally immersed in my own private thoughts, considering my hero beneath the burning sun in his warm-up suit, mimicking the ways of the monkey and the cobra. It was hard to believe that it could ever have happened, I repeated to myself. But it had! I had actually received a letter from a man whose physical prowess was legendary not only in Hong Kong but now in Hollywood as well! It was difficult not to permit a smile of triumph play upon my lips – especially when I looked over and saw the heaving, rocking figures within that self-styled assembly of critics whose greatest achievement in life appeared to be the acquisition of a 10p increase in their social security payments. Their shouts of 'Up Mullingar!' and 'Peking for the cup!' were as superannuated butterflies of sound carried off by the breeze as I strode out into the transformed evening.

*

The day I received the letter (Bruce! Lee! Each word seemed a fanfare of chimes!) saying that he would consider it a great honour and a privilege if I would allow him to be my guest one Saturday, I came close to fainting and was forced to support myself by clinging to the table's edge with my fingers. What still overcame me was the absolute perfection of his English! It was quite astounding! And, I reflected as I came back to myself, slowly releasing my thoughts – demolishing once and for all the cheap jibes such as 'Ah, sure, they can hardly write their name out there!' and 'You wouldn't expect to be able to read their writing, would you? Count yourself lucky if you get a few scribbles!', which were common currency in 'cosmopolitan' Barntrosna!

Which is the sort of small-town provincialism I find truly galling and beneath contempt. As if, just because you happen to be a lethal killing weapon capable of disposing of squadrons of sword-wielding, fright-wigged adversaries in two seconds flat, you are incapable of performing a simple task such as sitting down and writing a letter! Some hope! Instead what I would really like to see is some of these self-appointed protectors of the English language doing it! If, of course, they can manage to get the time off from that other important writing of theirs, which of course involves the weekly inscription of their dreary sobriquets on myriad unemployment benefit and assistance cheques.

No, as in everything else he did, his handwriting was fastidiously, scrupulously neat, and, like his well-aimed kicks to the midsection, contained no unnecessary strokes or embellishments of any kind. What he wished to say, he stated clearly and unambiguously. The question was, quite simply – would I be prepared to have him as my guest or not? The words floated before my eyes like beautiful nymphs preening themselves on a pavilion by a serene lake.

*

The day before my guest arrived, I was – I confess it! – hopelessly giddy and had barely sat down before I was up again, busying myself around the room plumping cushions and rearranging the maestro's books on the coffee table. As I have been collecting since the earliest years of my adolescence, I possess an extensive selection, titles including *Bruce Lee: Dragonmaster*, *Bruce the King*, *I Knew Bruce Lee*, *The Sword and the Snake – I Loved Bruce Lee* by Lung-Chi Wan, *Hong Kong Kickback – The Films of Bruce Lee*, *Bruce Lee – Why? – An Investigation into the Mysterious Death of a Martial Arts Genius* and some two or three hundred others I arranged about the various rooms. Which perhaps was overenthusiastic in retrospect, because by the time he arrived the front door opened only with great difficulty. I had arranged in advance for the Red Lotus Temple to deliver – direct to my residence! – their special set menu for two and it was piping away good and hot in the oven when the doorbell rang.

I must admit he was a little plumper and, indeed, somewhat taller, than I had imagined. But there could be no mistaking it – it was the high-flying crimefighter from the orient in all his glory. The charisma and sexuality that defined a proud, underdog masculinity confirmed that. He must surely have thought me a complete incompetent – I was so nervous! – as I dropped forks and repeated questions I had asked him heaven knows how many number of times! But, if this was the case, he graciously didn't show it. (I would have expected no less from him, to be truthful!) And when I brought in our serviettes and the steaming hot meal of chicken chow mein and pancake rolls, his eyes lit up as might a child's. 'Why! These are from the Red Lotus Temple!' he cried. I was flabbergasted. 'You mean – you know it?' I gasped. 'Oh but yes!' he replied. 'It is one of most famous Chinese restaurants in world!' I was thrilled beyond my wildest imaginings. I had been completely unaware of this fact!

How many topics we covered throughout the course of that little meal I cannot even begin to say. Suffice to observe that by the time we were finished there was little I did not know about the various protection rackets, Mafia heists and assorted 'stings' that go on around the world every day. The fascinating aspect of it all is that the more we talked, the more eager and interested – intoxicated, indeed – I became. 'Tell me, Bruce!' I began anew, when just at that precise moment, inexplicably, he began to laugh and actually spluttered some noodles down the front of his neatly tailored black jacket. On reflection, perhaps he wasn't laughing at all and one of the noodles became somehow lodged in his nostril, for there was nothing inherently amusing in my simple utterance of his name that I could see. In any case, I saw no point in drawing attention to it and continued with my question: 'Tell me, Bruce,' I said, 'do you see crime as a one-man personal vendetta brought on perhaps by something you witnessed as a child perhaps – the death of your parents at the hands of an unseen assailant, for instance – or is it something you feel you would have always wanted to pursue, regardless?' He thought for a moment, and then, lodging yet another noodle somehow in his nostril, he attempted to remove it, with the result that he coloured deeply, as a glittering moistness entered his eyes, a series of events culminating ultimately in the displacement of his plate and its entire contents which fell to the floor and arrayed themselves randomly about his feet, providing for both of us a situation which for a few brief moments was potentially very embarrassing indeed! But, fortunately, I remembered that I had, at the back of the refrigerator, one remaining Vesta Beef Curry which, I felt sure, if I cooked it swiftly and properly, would more than suffice to excite his palate. 'Don't worry, Bruce!' I cried. 'You haven't come all the way from Hong Kong to leave the McGeough house hungry! Oh no! Not by a long shot!' He found this quite amusing and signalled to me to stop as he lay down on the sofa and rubbed his moistened eyes with his world-famous, death-dealing hands.

To this day, I continue to congratulate myself on the presence of mind which I displayed on that occasion, for we continued then to have what I can only describe as the chat of a lifetime, what with Bruce not only agreeing to permit me to act as his official biographer and the chronicler of the story of our friendship which I felt was sure to blossom, but gratefully accepting from me modest donations to the Dragon of the Winged Tail Academy for those of slender means from the backstreets of Hong Kong who demonstrate at an early age their love of, and proven proficiency in, the martial arts. Those who complete their studies continue at another university just south of the city, where full training in cinema acting is given, with special visiting professors on hand to instruct the youthful crimefighters in the art of unpredictable and often seemingly incomprehensible dialogue which is so essential to the continuance of the preservation of law and order on the streets of the orient and to the endurance of such electrifying motion pictures as *He Kills Like A Bullet!* and *Die A Thousand Times!*.

I cannot begin to impart to you how overjoyed I was that night as I lay in my bed thinking over the events of the day. As I contemplated the intersecting, Mekong-style cracks in my ceiling, I could just imagine them in the Bridge Bar, seething with jealousy, practically about to self-combust such would be the insane fire of envy within them. It was difficult not to chuckle as I saw them there, perched on the stools like some forgotten human flotsam, the collars of their greatcoats turned up as they muttered: 'Look at McGeough! He thinks he's great! Just because he met Bruce Lee!'

Imprecise, I fear. No, I am not great. But neither am I – nor will ever be content to be – a peanut-munching, lotus-eating *Schadenfreude* peddler who lives on handouts from the state. That is a situation which shall never come to pass, for I shall ensure it. As I shall that whatever royalties I receive from my book – *Bruce Lee and Me* – shall never see the lining of my pocket but go straight to the Academy, via the kind auspices of the *Barntrosna Standard* Bruce Lee Fan Club PO Box which my friend has advised me to use as a cover lest the Mafia get wind of our little scheme. And which, I might add – according to the latest information available to me – is prospering wonderfully! Why, only last week, another impoverished Hong Kong boy cried *'Aiyahhh!'* triumphantly as he prepared to embark for Hollywood, sailing confidently through the air in his cotton pants, a helmet of ebony hair upon his head with a sheen of polish upon it so bright as to rival the Master.

As for the progress of the book itself, things are a little slower, for, as Bruce well knew, and shared with me so many times, no less than in the ancient art of kung fu patience is everything. And as regards the task on hand is absolutely of the essence, for I wish my story to be as near perfect as possible. To outline and candidly delineate not just the

47

background to my years of friendship with Bruce Lee but that of the martial arts as we have come to know them – the heists, the head-busting she-wolves, the drug lords, the torn trousers, the pieces of other films that get stuck in by accident. And until I have that story told to my satisfaction, I see no point in concerning myself unduly as to whether I receive the occasional letter from a publisher or not. Or, indeed, address-ing myself to the semi-intoxicated asides which show no signs of abating in the Bridge Bar, despite the fact that it is now over a decade since my first visit from the bard of the broken bone, and that rarely a day goes by without someone's hand being cupped and the query sailing forth from the shadows as to whether I've been in the Red Lotus lately. Not to mention assorted shadow-choppings, numerous 'Ha! Hatchas!' and wry asides casting doubt on the very existence of the Monkey School.

There was a time when I would, out of common decency and good manners, have acknowledged and attended to these veiled imputations. But no longer. My mind, I fear, is much too pre-occupied for that. First, there is my sealed envelope marked *Barntrosna Standard* and then there is my MS, with its neatly typed legend, *Bruce Lee and Me* (retitled), to be popped into a Jiffy bag addressed to my publishers in London. And, last but not least, there is my little cup of Chinese tea to drink – the best in all of Hong Kong (specially imported for me by the Red Lotus Temple) – before I retire, comfortably attired in my loose cotton pyjamas, to dream of youths who got a second chance and who, perhaps because of me and a man they called 'the Dragon', might one day course the Mao-red skies before landing with the force of a human grenade upon those who would dare to wage war upon his much-loved humanity, both Chinese and European, exultantly crushing every bone in their heads.

I Ordained the Devil

Now that I am approaching my seventieth year and consequently nearing the end of my ministry in the Church, I often get young curates coming up to me saying, 'Your grace, what was your most unforgettable experience in all your days as a minister in the one true Church?' or 'Of all the extraordinary events which have taken place over the years, my lord, which stands out most in your mind?'

Obviously, when such a question is put to one, immediately a multitude of images and memories come flooding into one's mind, like so many moths to the flame; that glorious day in the seminary in Maynooth, for example, when I myself was ordained; the occasion on which two of my colleagues were received by the Holy Father himself in the great city of Rome; the centenary of the college where I was educated and in which I once concelebrated Mass – the list is endless. Where to begin, dear reader? His grace swoons into a maelstrom of possibility.

Wiser perhaps to confine oneself to that question which is put with the greatest frequency, namely: 'Which was your truly most unforgettable, most traumatic experience?' Instantly that eliminates those days which have with the passage of time become suffused with an orange-amber glow and which, far from being traumatic, have served to act as a soothing palliative to the soul in troubled times.

But as each human being on this earth knows, and knows only too well, there are other days; suffused with no glow,

51

orange or amber or otherwise, but shot through with a pervading, monochromatic greyness, a sliver of which unyielding, ungenerous colourlessness, no matter what swirling obfuscating clouds one attempts to contrive as a protective shield or cloak, inevitably shines through. Yes, I have experienced such days in the course of my long career. Events have occurred which mean that, but for God's grace and the power of human prayer, I should not be sitting here today in this enormous Chesterfield chair, imbibing moderate sips of my Dubonnet and nibbling the occasional Ritz cracker so thoughtfully prepared for me by my housekeeper, Mrs Miniter. I should not be here today, girding myself to begin this tale – which to date I have related to but a single soul, a genial young student who visited me some months ago, keen to hear of my past experiences in a long and varied career. Initially, I was most reticent, but he was an intelligent young man, and his bright-eyed enthusiasm and eagerness eventually won me over. Yes, in the end I capitulated and told that young man, Hughie Turbot, the selfsame story I am about to relate here. Of how, as a young bishop in the diocese of Car and Clash, I ordained what I took to be a fresh, energetic young curate, well versed in both theology and pastoral care, champing at the bit to begin work with his flock in the parish of his birth, but who, in fact, turned out to be not remotely like that at all and to be in fact, the Horned One, the Beast, call him what you will – the Devil, in other words.

Of course, if I had advanced such a theory back then, in the dear glorious days beyond recall, when the students were arriving in droves at summer's end to begin the new term at St Mackie's Seminary, people would have said I had taken leave of my reason. 'What – Packie Cooley the Devil, your grace? I'm afraid you must have received a little too

much sun over the holidays!' And indeed, if I am honest, I
can genuinely see why they might have harboured such a
consideration. For on that first evening when I myself first set
eyes on him, just about the very last thing on my mind was
any notion that he might be the evil one. Yes, he was a
handsome lad indeed, young Packie, with a fistful of golden
copper curls that tumbled with some abandon across that
high polished forehead of his, and upon his lips that evening,
that bright – and to us, it seemed, entirely guileless – smile
to which we would soon become accustomed. No, the only
thing black about Packie Cooley in those days – precious
innocents! – was the spanking new soutane which his mother
had bought specially for him in a clerical outfitters in Dublin
and which flapped gaily about his legs as he chased the greasy
leather football across the moistened expanse of the junior
field, crying aloud with all the excitement of a young child:
'Ah, lads! Pass it to me, will youse, lads! Give me a welt of
it!' How we laughed when a near-superhuman effort on his
part to intercept – especially on damp days such as this –
the oft-recalcitrant orb as it made its way across the leaden
skies ended in disaster as he completely misjudged the path
of its trajectory and ended up face down in a very large patch
of sodden earth in the centre of the field which had the
consistency of the blancmange regularly served up to us for
dessert, and then raised himself up on his fists as best he
could, appearing for all the world as some kind of primeval
Mud-Man of whose exploits you might read in a child's
penny comic. Little did we know, of course – how could we
– that this was but an exasperatingly cunning ploy designed
to win our sympathies and affections – which it undoubtedly
did, for it is to that single incident the heart-warming cry
which was to become a feature of the college's corridors and

quadrangles, 'Good man, Packie!', may attribute its genesis. It was to be the first of a number of many conniving stratagems spawned for no reason other than to completely obliterate any suspicions that might attach themselves to the person of Packie Cooley and reveal his true identity – His Satanic Majesty, Diabolic Walker Among Men!

All of which were truly successful, for not once did the truth occur to myself, or my esteemed second-in-command in those days, Fr Buttkins McArdle. With whom I earnestly found myself in agreement when, having poured the Dubonnet for our nightcap one evening in my study, he angled his elbow and, leaning on the heavy marble mantelpiece, turned to me and with his eyes glittering, said: 'Do you know, your grace? I think the calibre of men we're getting is improving every year. I quizzed that young Packie Cooley up and down in Latin class and be cripes if he didn't come up trumps every time! As true as I'm standing here with my elbow on this mantelpiece, I don't think there's a Latin verb in the dictionary but he's conversant with it!'

Of course, if Buttkins were to say the exact same thing to me now, I know what my reply should be, ready and waiting to leap off my tongue. 'Aha!' I would cry. 'But do you know why that is, Buttkins? Because he is the Devil! And if the Devil is not knowledgeable in the art of the ancient languages, then I ask you – who is? Who is, I ask you!'

But Fr McArdle isn't here today, of course, having thrown himself off the roof of St Mackie's some years ago in the throes of a mid-life crisis concerning the validity of his faith and his relationship with his Maker, and so my words are as wishful thinking, nothing more. And the truth is, dear reader, that the reply which I made to my gentle deceased friend and colleague in faith on that occasion long ago was: 'Packie Cooley is as brainy a scholar as ever strode through the portals of St Mackie's, Father. And as far from committing the sin of pride as Castlebar is from Dingle.' And to which my old friend, tilting the meniscus of his dark beverage, mused softly: 'Now you've said it. You've said it now and no mistake, me old butty!'

I would soon come to rue those words! How can I begin to impress upon you, dearest reader, how it galls me to this day to think that I, who had been – not a rock! but a virtual *slab* of *granite* to my beloved students, should have been deceived by the smiling cherubic complexion of a football-playing 'angel' whose heart seemed to burst with passion for both his peers and the human race in general. But who, in truth, was the leavings of the celestial barrel, a handful of Mephistophelian scrapings whose soul was as nothing more than a piece of canine excrement you might tread underfoot when you were pacing the perimeter of the football field in the company of your colleagues at the end of a long teaching day. Surely, dear readers, even amongst the fallen themselves there must prevail some form of hierarchy. One must surely believe that even within the breast of the wickedest succubus there gleams some tiny star of hope, of goodness.

*

But not within that of Packie Cooley. For, as it gradually and inevitably became clear to me, he was no unspectacular drone in the armies of Hades. Would that he had been! Would that he had, gentle reader!

By now, I feel certain that it is evident as to why these reminiscences continue to trouble me so. Had Packie Cooley been nothing more than a humdrum private in those black, smoking regiments of the expelled, perhaps there might have been a tiny glimmer of the hope of which I have spoken earlier. But what I didn't realize – along with the fact that it was by now already too late to do anything even if I had! – was that I was dealing with no casual, insouciant, part-time agent of the shadows. What I now harboured within the walls of my beloved seminary – which I would have realized had he not so effectively fashioned winkers for me with his – as I now can see it – reptilian charm – was the very President of the Damned, the Earl of Nothingness – Satan himself!

*

The first indication I had that Fr Packie Cooley might not exactly be who he said he was came on a dark night in the year 1961, not long after the terrible news had arrived that some Irish soldiers had been brutally done to death by members of the marauding Baluba tribe in the Congo region of Africa. I had just concluded my spiritual reading and was making my way along the main corridor to my room when I became aware of a presence close by, and upon turning the corner leading to what was affectionately known as the Big Corridor, to my astonishment found the student in question (he was by now a subdeacon) chuckling away to himself as he held the newspaper, as large tears coursed down his flushed, excessively mobile face, spattering the newsprint of the paper which he held before him. 'Packie,' I gasped, 'oughtn't you be in bed?' 'Yes,' he coughed as he began his reply, 'but I was so upset at this dreadful news that I simply couldn't sleep. Did you read about it yourself, Father? You know what they did to those poor soldiers, don't you? They ate them! It's beyond words! It's just too much to bear!'

With that, he covered his face with his black-clad arm and

fled down the corridor, the echo of his muffled sobs lingering in the silence long after he had left the building.

Had that been all, it is likely that I should have thought no more of it, but when I examined the newspaper – which in his 'distressed' state he had discarded on the window ledge – I noted that onto the image of one of the unfortunate deceased military had been added a crudely drawn pair of spectacles and ludicrously thin moustache, and beneath that again, a barely legible scrawl which formed the words – my head lightened – *Irish stew! It's tasty!*

The strangest of feelings enveloped me as I stood there in the half-light of evening, as if a ghost-snake were making its way with infinite but lithe patience up and down the length of my spine. The tragedy is that I did not acknowledge the import of this sign, shot through with foreboding as it most surely was, but simply shook myself and folded up the newspaper, popping it into the waste-paper basket as I proceeded on my way to the Sacred Heart dormitory.

The next incident took place in the sacristy on the 11th of November 1962 when I was doffing my vestments, having completed my celebration of Mass. I was in quite high spirits – it was a truly beautiful morning, with spears of golden sunlight seeming to impishly fence with each other above the mosaic in that bright and airy room – and was looking forward to my religious instruction class with my students, humming '*Juxta crucem! Misericordiae!*' quite absentmindedly, I have to admit, when I perceived at my feet a most extraordinary sight. Initially, the opinion that I formed of this spectacle was that it was but random flecks of foam perhaps dislodged from the jaws of a hastily shaved, unfortunately tardy colleague, but I was forced to revise this – an unjustifiably hasty assumption in any case – almost immediately when I realized that what my eyes were gazing upon were nothing other than the tiniest fragments of printed paper. But not only that – for what lay beneath me, on those polished tiles, were pieces removed from the most holy missal! My perplexity deepened. Who could have done this thing? I asked of myself again and again, turning the fragments – some of them actually compressed until they had become hard pellets – abstractedly in my hands. It was then I looked up to see him standing there above me – Packie Cooley. Instinctively one is alert to the mysterious energies which often pass between human beings. An intense current which can be revelatory, combining now with a grey nimbus of cloud which seemed to form itself like a mask before his eyes, veiling his normally fresh complexion as if to say: 'The man you are looking upon is not Packie Cooley! For he has ceased to be that man!'

By this point I was emotionally overwrought. I cast my eyes over the tattered remnants of what had once been a beautifully hand-stitched gold-embossed religious book and cried: 'Who could have done this? Who?' Then – gloriously, in a way, weakening, I became aware at that very moment of his stifled yet unmistakable sobbing, and felt his comforting hand fall upon my shoulder, as he said: 'Now more than ever the Church needs us, Father. There is no knowing the extent to which our enemies and the enemies of the one true established Church will go.' Flushed as I was, in my heady emotional state, I found myself clasping his hand – idiotically, as is now only all too evident – and, as if I had been personally and single-handedly responsible for snatching a soul in danger from the trapdoor that led to the Pit itself, cried aloud: 'Yes, Packie! It's so true! What you say is so, so true!'

Instead – if only I had done it! – of slapping him across the face and crying: 'Don't lie, you hypocrite! You did this! You did it, Cooley! You! And for one reason and one alone! Because you're the Devil and it's your job!'

But, whether or not through the gathering of so many anxieties within me like so many atomic gases, it was not to be, and I feel no pride, readers, none at all as I look back upon it, that half-hour in an early morning sacristy where we stand together, collecting ill-fitting pieces of creased and irretrievably torn tissue paper, Sellotaping and aligning them, those forlorn fragments, as best we could into an approximation of what that sad, blasphemed publication had once been.

Many times since have I reflected that had I acted on either of those two occasions – it is with tormented soul and guilt-drenched heart I have picked up Conrad's tales of guilt and cowardice in the face of adversity, I assure you! – perhaps the scorch-footed march of the fork-tongued soul-taker would have been halted. But it was not to be! My eyes were as blind as those of a bat long since in thrall to the demon grape, the pail from the well of moral courage drawn up once more, hopelessly empty, as the career of 'Fr Packie Cooley' proceeded apace, nay hurtled.

*

First there was the medal for Best Student. Then followed the Essay of 1963 award, and of course Exemplary Latin and Classics Scholar of the same year. Not to mention the captaining of the team which sailed to victory in the 1965 Cardinal McGing All-Ireland Championships trophy. On a morning in 1967, I opened a copy of *Caritas* magazine to discover once more his sleek, Brylcreemed head superimposed above the squat, many-windowed outline of a fever hospital which, apparently, he had single-handedly been responsible for building in the African parish where he was finishing up as spiritual administrator, having been transferred home – I shuddered! – to the town of Barntrosna, in the parish of Clonacoosey. All of a sudden I was seized by a blind, uncontrollable panic. Some inexplicable, atavistic fury found me with the magazine twisted beyond all recognition in my lap. What am I to do? I repeated hoarsely to myself as I paced the Axminster of my study. Never in the history of St Mackie's had the rise of a student been so meteoric. It was at that point – yet another fever-sweltering dream concerning my failure to act on that fateful morning in the sacristy having wakened me in the night – I became convinced that events were definitely coming to a head with Mr Packie 'Fr' Cooley!

I flung the remains of *Caritas* magazine into the waste-paper basket and resolved at once to act.

*

I arrived at St Ignatius's General Hospital (in which establishment I had ascertained he had taken up residence as chaplain) on the morning of the 16th of July 1967, to be informed, to my amazement, that 'Dear Fr Packie' had had his farewell party only the evening before and was now stationed in the town of Labacusha, fifty-five miles south of Drogheda. Little did I know that on the very spot where I stood, only one year later fifteen children would be wheeled out on squeaking trolleys, each and every one of them having perished from some inexplicable, unidentified illness – and each of them members, at one time or another, of Fr Packie Cooley's St Ignatius's Hospital Soldiers of Christ Choral and Drama Group.

Those, of course, were the days of flower power and 'hippies' and the strains of popular hits of the time, dealing as they did with young people opting out of society and what have you, delivered up their raucous, hopelessly deluded cacophony to the street as I made my way past some elderly cap-doffing citizens, struggling with the defiantly atonal strains of ludicrously foreign instruments in an effort to gather my thoughts and formulate some plan of action.

I am not and have never pretended to be a cleric in the G. K. Chesterton mould, but conscious as I was of the importance and, at this juncture, undoubted urgency of my task, I gave myself wholeheartedly to the investigation and within a matter of mere days had located the elusive, chameleon-like clergy-man. A young boy I chanced to encounter in the supermarket told me that it was his custom to attend the 'cubs' with 'Fr Packie' and that if I was to make my way on Thursday evenings to the vicinity of the local football field, I would without a doubt find him there.

*

To this day, any recollection of the sight that met my eyes on that fateful day in 1967 as I briskly turned the corner towards the football field fills me with an almost intolerable grief. For there, ringed by a phalanx of red-eyed young boys in shorts who were sobbing their little hearts out, was the prone figure of an eight-year-old, now lying dead on the grass because of a 'kick in the head'. An 'unfortunate, freakish accident', it would later, in the full throes of his weeping, be categorized by the 'trainer' – who, of course, was none other than . . .!

I fled from that place, lest I become overwrought and find myself drawn into physical confrontation, which could only – in those maddeningly fabricated circumstances – have proved counter-productive. Being possessed, of course, of no concrete proof of what were not – at this stage – my suspicions, but my absolute convictions, I could not feasibly make my accusations public, crying: 'I know, Cooley! I know, you see! You've played your last card here, my friend!' or similar. And thus I was compelled to bide my time and enjoin the Lord to continue to assist me as I gave myself wholeheartedly to my investigations which I realized would now have to become both dogged and persistent if there was to be any hope of confounding my adversary, which he now undoubtedly and most emphatically was, for who can look upon the pale cold countenance of a once-breathing footballing child in the prime of his youth without a sliver of ice entering their heart?

Following the 'sad incident', as the credulous local newspaper described the passing of little Tommy McGinnity, the parish priest – Ladies! Have you met Fr Lucifer? He'll be taking over from Fr Joe! Ha ha! – retired to Europe for a short holiday, returning prematurely when the city of Paris was torn apart by riots – the photographs of which, as has now become common knowledge (at least among us, the clergy, much as it horrifies us to admit it), revealed, without exception, the unmistakable figure of a familiar white-collared silhouette, its face disfigured by pure evil.

I was horrified to hear that on his return he had been appointed pastor of St Gertie's School for Girls, a reputable convent on the south side of Dublin City. Rather than make my presence conspicuous, I decided to employ a more peripheral modus operandi, attiring myself after the manner of a gardener in a tweed hat and weather-beaten brown corduroys, and applying for the position which I had been given to understand was currently available there. And which, I am happy to say, having acquainted myself with all manner of domestic plants and flowers which might have been expected to be found thriving there, I am happy to say I was successful in acquiring.

With small three-pronged fork in hand, my investigations were now to begin in earnest.

*

The shriek of what at other times might reasonably have been considered girlish laughter echoing in the night to this day returns to haunt me, and with it the memory of fit young bodies appearing at unadorned windows like pure, unblemished dolls only to be whisked away by a cackling shape with unmistakably protruding horns. Which I endured as best I could, but in the end I could take no action other than that which I did, bursting into his office, firmly slamming a paperweight upon the felt-topped desk as I cried, hoarsely, such was the level of my distress: 'The Devil is in this building!'

But little did I realize – even yet! – the adroitness and resourcefulness of the fiendish intelligence with which I was now engaged. Some days later, subsequent to the 'exhaustive' interviews she had conducted with him – a consequence of my relentless insistence – I was horrified to hear Sister Soobie inform me that far from discovering the 'can of worms the like of which the ecclesiastical world can only have nightmares about' she had now come to the conclusion that my accusations regarding Fr Packie were nothing short of 'hysterical', which, as it transpired, the reverend mother did too, remarking coolly as she sipped her tea, 'Can you imagine! Our Fr Packie!'

I will not pretend that I found myself in any place but the pits of despair as I doffed my tweed hat for the last time and slipped quietly down the avenue, not once turning to look back, the black energy that was radiating from behind the glass where he stood at the main window of the reception room on the ground floor, along with the catgut-thin length of his lopsided, teasing grin, just about as much as I could at that moment humanly bear.

It is of little use now to repeat that only days later the carcass of a sacrificed sheep was discovered in one of the girls' wardrobes and that a secret compartment in the senior locker room gave up its horrid contents of bales of pornographic magazines and an upside-down cross.

There is an old folk-tale dating back to famine times, that in places where the dreaded blight exhaled its foul, dread breath, it was found when it had passed that in each of these stricken villages there was somehow always a locked cottage. Locked, firmly shuttered, and seemingly uninhabited. Inexplicable yes, but a constant which remained with dogged ferocity throughout those shoot-rotting, nettle-munching days, on each and every occasion when the blank, unfeeling door was broken in, revealing the interior to be packed floor to ceiling with what can only be described as a ridiculous surfeit of foodstuffs, including potatoes, corn, maize and any number of handsomely filled wooden chests of Indian tea. Not uncommon also were sides of cooked ham. All of which, of course, had mysteriously disappeared only weeks before the ragged cloak of the hunger had first draped itself about the unwitting land! Is there any need for me to point out the single, stark and unequivocal conclusion which we have no choice but to draw from these assembled, totally incontrovertible facts? That in each of these unfortunate villages at that time, there had resided and 'ministered' a man known by only one name – Mr Packie 'Fr' Cooley!

And thus it came as no surprise whatsoever to me when, almost a year to the day after my experiences in Labacusha, I picked up the newspaper to enjoy a relaxing read after a very pleasant evening meal – (lovely buns!) – prepared for me as usual by the ever-reliable Mrs Miniter, and, once again, felt the blood begin to drain from my face as I discerned before my very eyes – in shimmering black bold type, such once more were the levels of my gathering anxieties – the words STRANGE GOINGS-ON IN COUNTY CORK VILLAGE, and composed myself as best I could to assimilate the bizarre details of the story as they unfolded before me. By all accounts, the local bank had been robbed no less than eleven times, and it appeared that of late beer and marijuana parties had become a regular occurrence in the town, but not clandestinely hidden away in some seemingly respectable suburb behind discreet Venetian blinds but in full view of the inhabitants as they went about their daily chores – on the village green itself! One youth when interviewed stated baldly that he did not care what the police or the priests said and that he was going to do his 'own thing' whether they liked it or not. A beautiful-looking young girl with all her life before her saw absolutely nothing wrong, it would seem, with brashly pronouncing that it was her express intention to earn her living by becoming a common prostitute as soon as she was old enough to take her leave of the village. As if this wasn't enough, a roughneck who smugly described himself as a 'Hell's Angel' magnanimously shared with the world the edifying information that nothing would give him quite so much pleasure as any occasion, in any public place or private establishment whatsoever (he was not choosy, he informed us), which might provide him with an opportunity to, as he quaintly termed it, 'bust heads'. Behind this explosion of poorly tended face-fungus and unkempt leather, I gloomily noted the outline of a blazing building, which valiant firemen were doing their level best to quench.

By the time I made for my bed, there was little doubt in my mind as to who was behind this latest manifestation of creeping entropy or whatever label one might care to put on it, and a few well-placed telephone calls the following morning only served to confirm my worst suspicions. It transpired that Cooley had been transferred from a violence-ridden hamlet in the west (where faction-fighting, unknown for generations, had erupted again with a vengeance – 1,300 people being hospitalized over one two-day period) to this unfortunate, selfsame village only weeks before! As I replaced the receiver, my heart beat in my chest like a bellows and the blood coursed through my palpitating veins like some veritable crashing Niagara. Cigarette upon cigarette I smoked, pacing the Axminster and cracking my knuckles until even the mild-mannered Mrs Miniter could take no more and cried: 'Stop that! Stop that, your grace! Stop it now, I tell you!'

I apologized profusely to her and seated myself in my Chesterfield as at last I felt a cool, refreshing calm descending over me. A cool calm that whispered: 'This time you'll have to act. You know that, your grace – don't you?'

It is not with any pride I report that barely five minutes after my foot touched the surface of the main street of Bunacash, in the county of Cork, I found myself propositioned by a gum-chewing teenager in a blouse or shirt so flimsy that it barely seemed to exist at all, who promised to show me one or two things I would have only read about in books, and it was all – God forgive me! – I could do not to slap her face right there and then to bring her back to her senses as I held her against the wall and cried: 'What is going on here! Who put you up to this!' But I could see that she was so high on drugs that I would succeed in prising no information of any worth out of her. I knew there was nothing for it but to make straight for the presbytery to confront my quarry once and for all. Discarding my shrieking, giddy charge, I hastily gathered my skirts about me and stormed uncompromisingly down the main street.

I was heartened by my firm sense of purpose and resolution, or at least I understood myself to be until I flung the front door of the presbytery open and there to my horror beheld what I had long feared and suspected – a sight so repellent that I can scarcely bring myself to describe it here. There, before my very eyes, draped across the chaise longue – like some hideous oriental puzzle of flesh – in a pose which can only be described as 'grotesque' and exuding a seductive lotus-eating lassitude, were any number of nubile young women in various states of undress, blearily laughing their heads off and clearly under the influence of some soporific narcotic. Enthusing pathetically as the Devil himself, sporting a clerical collar but bereft of any other form of human garb or clothing of any kind, blasphemed wildly as he sprang wildly about the room in an abominable, mocking gavotte, his smoking manhood lividly erect before him. 'Say you worship me, my sweet ones!' I heard him cackle. 'Worship for ever He Who Destroys!'

The sight of those once innocent eyes as they slid to the floor before him was more than I could bear. 'NO!' I cried, leaping into the air and catching him firmly by the horns, falling across the coffee table (upon which were casually discarded any number of glossy magazines happily displaying further preposterously interlocking combinations of pink-hued female flesh). I – from whence I found my strength to this day I do not know – I began to pummel him furiously without restraint about his charcoal-coloured razor-toothed visage, crying hysterically – for it is no lie – I was close to losing my reason – 'No, Cooley! No more, you hear me! You have destroyed enough lives! This for you is the end of the road! Do you hear me? Do you hear me – Emperor of Hell!' With all the resources I could humanly muster, I continued to lay forcefully about him, using his horns as a grip whilst I brought his head into contact with the floor. Had he been but human my work would, within minutes have been complete. But Packie Cooley was not human. Indeed, he was so far from that condition that the mortal mind can only begin to imagine it, as I discovered when I looked up from my handiwork only to find, with a gradually growing sickening sensation of hopelessness, that he was standing virtually unscathed adjacent to the drinks cabinet sipping a brightly coloured viscous liquid, as though some deranged lounge-lizard, enquiring with one raised eyebrow as to whether I was finished yet. Such was the feeling of despair – not to mention physical exhaustion – that my head slumped lifelessly to my chest and I could bear no more of his understated taunts, his limp-wristed, degenerate admonitions to the now reassembling pyramid of alabaster-pale flesh, whose laughter accelerated inside my mind as I lay there, prone and red-eyed, ineffectual, empty, for all to see. As in a dream, I perceived them begin to advance upon me, the irregular cracks upon the white ceiling slowly converging as his razor teeth shone, his grey fingers approaching as if to stroke my cheek towards Hades and the eternal boatman, the only recollection remaining to me, consumed as I was now with exhaustion and – to my shame! – naught but a longing for oblivion, being that of my soutane's forcible removal and the Prince of Blackness standing over me, rubbing his night-dark hands with glee as the transformed figures – for they surely must once have been women – cavorted, shrieking, waving their arms as they

68

gleefully inhaled lungfuls of the purplish smoke that by now had filled the room.

*

When I awoke, all was silent once more, for they had vanished and everything was in its place as if I had somehow wandered into an establishment which, with the absolute minimum of effort on the part of anyone, would somehow always succeed in garnering first prize in any presbytery-of-the year competition. It was absolutely immaculate. As I composed myself, I endeavoured to piece together the series of events which had led to my abandonment in a totally unfamiliar environment, flushed and soutane-less, and was succeeding to some extent in piecing together the many ill-fitting components of the jigsaw when suddenly I became aware of a sealed cream manila envelope at my elbow, which I opened with trembling hands. I had good reason, as I within moments began to realize, to feel apprehensive, for the contents of that envelope fashioned for me a prison which, albeit with invisible bars, would soon prove itself to be as impregnable an Alcatraz or any high-security place of incarceration as those of a fiercely custodial frame of mind have yet to dream up. For the words which I read upon that fine, unstained stationery informed me – with not the slightest hint of equivocation – that if I 'made the slightest attempt' to 'follow his "Nocturnal Grace" ever again' – and here I experienced a particular frisson of arctic coldness, for the word 'ever' was both italicized and in bold type – he would have no hesitation in activating the diabolic genes which he and his 'lady friends' had implanted within me as I slept, the consummate consequence of which would be that, helpless to prevent myself, I would find myself running amok in the streets and villages of Ireland, murdering people, robbing and looting shops, selling drugs and burning down churches and people's houses. So, his eerie scrawl concluded (even it too seemed redolent of anthracite), if I had any sense, I would know what to do and remain for quite a sizeable portion of the foreseeable future where I belonged – safely within the confines of the Bishop's Palace, with my mouth securely shut.

*

His career since that awful night has been handsomely productive. Rarely a day goes past but someone is shot or pitchforked and only yesterday £150 million worth of narcotics was discovered in Newtownburkett. Occasionally I will switch on the television to find him confronting me once more, discoursing freely on the topic of 'young people' and describing with tented fingers how he considers Jesus to be his 'special friend'. At times like that it is all I can do not to weep or put my carpet slipper through the screen. For I know that no matter what I do, or what labyrinthine plan of action I formulate, it is clear that I have been trumped. How can I pretend it to be otherwise when he has implanted within me what can only be described as the equivalent of a nuclear time bomb? Even worse, he has, through some form of hypnosis, succeeded in convincing many of my fellow clergymen that I am jealous of him and that it is for this reason and this alone I had been spending my time spreading the wickedest of rumours, and slandering his name at every available opportunity. At various conferences, I have become aware of this innuendo – mutterings of 'mad because of his popularity' and 'because he hasn't it in him himself, you see' spring to mind. It is with a heavy heart I acknowledge that such asides and corner-of-the-mouth insinuations persist to this day. Only last week, it was my misfortune to overhear a colleague assert his opinion that 'having got the bishopric you'd think he'd have enough without bad-mouthing a good priest like Packie Cooley'. There can be little doubt but that he has succeeded in performing his work well. The talk of him succeeding me here in the palace (his sights ultimately being set upon the highest ecclesiastical office in the land, of course!) has already begun and rarely a night goes by but I envisage him leering at me from the corner of the room, waving coyly as he adjusts the red silk cape and rakishly tilts his cardinal's hat. And thus it is destined to continue – there is an infuriating inevitability about it! – night after night until (to begin with!), he has himself firmly ensconced here by the fireside, with Mrs Miniter innocently providing him with scones and teacake as she once did me.

No, for me there is no option now but to bite my lower lip and pass on. Pass on, my only company on the solitudinous peregrinations that are to be my lot. Heavily – unbearably – burdened within by the sad knowledge that only I possess. The sad knowledge that the most influential clergyman in all of Ireland today is none other than the Devil himself and, even sadder still, knowing in my episcopal heart and soul that, for every drug addict and degenerate sex baron brazenly disporting themselves about streets once a paradigm for all civilized society, there is no one to be deemed responsible but me.

After all, readers – I ordained the fucker.

The Hands of Dingo Deery

For many years I have lived alone, within the four grey walls of this narrow room, the tremulous silence intermittently broken by the tube trains which cut through the tar-black night with their cargo of ghostly, pallid faces, as if in relentless, heartbroken pursuit of something lost a long time ago, just as the peaceful harmony which once pervaded my entire being has been bitterly wrested from me.

How many years have I paced these accursed floorboards, imploring any deity who cares to listen to return to me the bountiful tranquillity which once was mine and end for ever this dread torment which greets me like a rapacious shade each waking day!

And now, as I stand here by the window, watching with leaden, emotion-drained eyes, directly below me, a single line of mocking, waltzing calligraphy; at last they confront me, the jagged ciphers which, all this time, I have feared would one day rise up from my blackest dreams like wicked flares from the pit of hell: THE SECRETS OF LOUIS LESTRANGE: CAN YOU SURVIVE THE 1,137 WHACKS???

*

My nightmare began some thirty years ago in a small town in Ireland, not far from Mullingar and quite near Dundalk. I had come to Barntrosna to spend the summer with my uncle, who was the headmaster in the local school. He had of late acquired some measure of fame as an ornithologist and it gave me great pleasure indeed to accompany him on his regular lectures in various halls and venues throughout the county. It is not my intention to imply that my duties were in any way onerous for, in truth, beyond the simple erection of the screen and the operation of the slide projector, there was little for me to do. I carried the briefcase containing my learned relative's notes, it is true, but such was his erudition that he made little use of what he termed 'needless paraphernalia', and it was of such insignificant weight that it could have been comfortably borne to the Temperance Hall (in which establishment it was his practice to deliver his orations on the habits of our feathered friends) on the back of the average housefly. What a privilege it was for me to turn the metal disc yet another semicircle as, in basso profundo, he would declaim, 'Slide, please!' while his neighbours and friends looked on admiringly.

As I look back on those days now, they always seem to me suffused with the colour of burnished copper and within them time does not appear to move at all.

Afterwards I would stroll casually through the cooling streets, making the acquaintance of the elderly gentlemen who whiled away their hours on the Summer Seat discussing the imminent ruin of the country and the hypothetical prowess of assorted thoroughbreds in contests that had yet to be.

I would regularly share a lemonade with them, perhaps on occasion pass around a packet of Player's. Laughter and an unbending faith in the goodness of our fellow man was a common bond amongst us all, and there was little doubt in my mind that where I had the good fortune to find myself was indeed the most idyllic town on earth. And had you taken it upon yourself to share your intimations that darker times would soon be discerned on the horizon, I would have extrapolated from your spurious, clandestine misanthropy nothing more than a bitter, small-minded and wholly despicable envy. I should have evinced scorn and packed you off about your business. For if ever a truth were spoken, it was that evidence of dissension in that sweet little hamlet there was none. Save perhaps the awesome figure of a well-known layabout by the name of Dingo Deery, who at odd intervals would appear wild-eyed in the doorway of the hall and bellow at the top of his voice: 'Shut your mouth, Lestrange! What would you know about it! You wouldn't know a jackdaw if it walked up to you and pecked your auld whiskey nose off!' Whereupon he would spread his arms and assail the stunned, mute assembly: 'You think he knows about birds? He knows nothing! Except how to beat up poor unfortunate scholars for not knowing their algebra! Look at these hands! Look at them, damn youse!'

When he had spoken these words, he would break into a sort of strangled weeping and raise his palms aloft, and indeed there were few present who could deny on first viewing those bruised pieces of flesh that they undoubtedly had seen wear and tear beyond reasonable expectation, even for someone of his social standing. 'Cut to ribbons!' he would cry hoarsely. 'Cut to ribbons by Lestrange! Him and his sally rods! Oho yes – you were handy with them all right, Lestrange! But mark my words, you'll pay for what you did to Dingo Deery – I can tell you that!' Then, with a maniacal cackle, his recalcitrant, cumbersome bulk would be forcibly ejected, the distasteful echo of his combative ululations lingering in the air for long afterwards.

But such incidents were indeed rare, and otherwise life proceeded serenely: Yuri Gagarin was in space, Player's cost one and six and John Fitzgerald Kennedy was undoubtedly the possessor of the cleanest teeth in the Western hemisphere.

It was to be many years before the arrival of colour television and the first drug addicts.

*

The first day I met Mick Macardle, I knew instinctively all was not as it should have been. Deep within me, I heard a timorous voice cry: 'Withdraw! Withdraw while you still can!' The languid sunshine, however, and the soothing breeze of the early afternoon conspired in silence to usher away any such uncharitable and unnecessary suspicions.

But now, as I languish here in my one-room prison, forgotten in a city which remembers no names, my heart has crusted over and no such beguiling veils remain to blur my vision, and with staggering clarity I see what ought to have met my eyes in those days of benevolence-blinded myopia, a sight which, had I not been poked in those organs by two large metaphorical thumbs, should surely have swept through my soul like an arctic wind.

The thin cigar hung insolently out of the side of his mouth. A black raven's wing of Brylcreemed hair fell ominously down over his alabaster forehead. His lips were two ignominious pencil strokes, his moustache not unlike a crooked felt-tipped marker line as it might be drawn by a small child. More than anything, however, what ought to have telegraphed to me the imponderable depth of the man's reptilian nature was the slow slither of his arm about my shoulder, the hiss of his silky sibilants as he crooned into my ear: 'Don't worry about a thing!' Then, out of nowhere, he would erupt into inexplicable torrents of laughter, the flat of his hand repeatedly falling on the broad of my back as he cried: 'You leave it to Mick! I'll take care of it!'

'No prob!' he would cry, sawing the noun in two like some cheapskate magician in a tawdry show.

How I should have loathed the man! But no – my innocence and desire to think the best of all fellows won the day, and even when he passed by my uncle's house in his new Ford Consul, waving through the open window like a visiting dignatory from a Lilliputian puppet state, I chose to ignore the unspoken counsel of my instinct, preferring instead to align myself with the views of those citizens of the town who ranged themselves about him, some indeed claiming kinship, as they declared him 'one fine butt of a lad!' and insisting furthermore that there was 'no better man in this town!'

The abrupt nasal-spurt of his megaphone could be heard far and wide as his glittering Consul zigzagged through the candy-striped streets of summer. 'Yes!' it would bark with metallic brio. 'Yes, ladies and gentlemen! Mick Macardle for all your movie requirements! Why not drop along to Mac's Photography Shop at number 9 Main Street? Come along and see what we have to offer! Weddings, christenings, confirmations! Never be negative with Mick Macardle! Mick Macardle's the movie man! No prob! Yes, siree!'

Thus life proceeded. The church bells would ring out across the morning town, the womenfolk give themselves once more to the fastidious investigation of vegetables and assorted foodstuffs in the grocery halls, brightening each other's lives with picaresque travelogues of failing innards and the more recent natural disasters, delaying perhaps at the corner to engage in lengthy discourse with Fr Dominic, their beloved pastor. 'That's not a bad day now,' they would observe, the clergyman as a rule finding himself in fulsome agreement. 'Indeed and it is not,' he would respond enthusiastically, occasionally a dark cloud of uncertainty passing across his fresh, close-shaven features as he added: 'Although I think we might get a touch of rain later!'

Observations of similar perspicacity would provide a further ten minutes of eager debate before they would once more proceed on their way, past Grouse Armstrong snuggled up in the library doorway, the single American tourist snapping gypsies in the hotel foyer ('Couldja throw a little more grit on your heads, guys?') and Sonny Leonard the local minstrel rehearsing 'I wonder who's kissing her now' into the neck of the brown bottle which served as his microphone.

Sadly, even at that transcendent moment, as I gave my heartiest approval to the maestro's impromptu recital with rousing cheers of 'Good man, Sonny!' and 'More power to your elbow, young Leonard!', disturbing events were already proceeding as the sleek limousine bearing Mick Macardle cruised silently through the streets of Amsterdam, the Barntrosna businessman seated comfortably now by the side of an ambitious, long-fingered entrepreneur, a sinister individual of foreign complexion who, within hours (I know it! Despite assertions – and there have been some! – that it is mere conjecture and foolish rambling on my part! For I, Dermot Mooney, am no erratic, fevered fantasist, and never have been! I scorn such pathetic and perjorative imputations!), would be outlining his proposition in an outwardly unremarkable lock-up garage, its dimly lit interior, however, festooned with tattered pictures of young ladies in abbreviated attire, helpless females of tender years being pursued by villains of the wickedest mien sporting pork-pie hats – you can be certain of it! – their misfortunate quarries crying helplessly from the suspended cages in which they ultimately found themselves.

Forced to become slit-skirted temptresses leering through uncoiling cobras of smoke, captured for ever in calligraphic captivity as the houndstooth letters whorled all about them in a dizzying, soporific swirl! That same houndstooth lettering that would later choke my soul in bondage like so many miles of barbed wire: *Evil Virgin Thrills! Runaway Go-Go Psychos! I Married Hitler!*

*

Despicable memories which course through me like a slow-acting poison, the very thought of my uncle and me adorning that Gallery of the Damned like an eerie step across my grave.

*

Mick Macardle – I can picture the scene as though it were being choreographed before my very eyes, for I know these people! – tapped one-eighth of an inch of ash from his thin cigar as the Dutchman ran his tongue along his upper teeth and fanned his fingers on the oil-stained tabletop. 'Very well, Mr Macardle,' he began, 'that arrangement suits me fine. For each copy you deliver on time, you will receive the sum of five hundred pounds sterling. However I must emphasize that I can only accept eight-millimetre as the films are for private distribution. I cannot emphasize how keen my clients are for this type of product and you may rest assured that demand will constantly outstrip supply. Do you feel you may be able to rise to meet the demands, Mr Macardle?'

To which the brown-suited businessman responded – undoubtedly – by paring the nail of his index finger with a marbled pocket knife, flashing his gold tooth and grinning: '*No prob!*'

With one wave of his Woolworth's wand began my Golgotha.

To the poor, glorious but innocent souls of the town he had not been on an evil, self-seeking mission which was soon to shatter for ever the harmony that existed amongst us all, but merely, as he cheerfully volunteered: 'Visiting the mother in Dundalk! She has a bad dose of the shingles!'

As was their wont in time of difficulty, the commiserations of the local people knew no bounds. Their admiration of such forbearance as he displayed in his time of trial was deep and respectful. 'How do you manage to keep going at all?' they enquired of him. 'Ah,' he would reply, with a modest shake of his head, 'I have great faith in St Anthony!'

Thus my genial life proceeded – setting up the screen, making tea for the various societies, who never failed to be impressed by my uncle's oratory, his statesmanlike imperturbability displaying any hint of fragility only on those occasions when the door would burst open and a familiar figure appear, crying: 'I'll give you *Cicinurrius regius*! I'll give you turquoise-billed yellow-jacket! I'll give you long-necked hoppa tail! Look at these hands, Lestrange! One day you'll pay for what you did to me! Make no mistake, you'll pay all right!'

It was also my custom in those days to dine occasionally at an establishment known as the Pronto Grill, which was presided over by a gentleman of Italian extraction who busied himself singing selections from the various light operas and furiously polishing drinking glasses. Over a sumptuous repast magnificently prepared by the kitchen staff, to whom I had become affectionately known as More Tay!, because of my predilection for consuming inordinate quantities of the soothing, tan-coloured liquid with my meal, I watched life proceed before me in the warm street outside, at times fearing that such was my ecstatic state I might collapse in a faint on the formica table before me.

For, in truth, it was not the exquisite quality of the comestibles alone that drew me to my quiet cove adjacent to the streaming chrome of the coffee machine, but the soft voices of the young convent ladies who would converge there in the afternoons, rapt in their sophistry and circumscribing elongated shapes in the spilt sugar.

Perhaps I had consumed inadvisable quantities of 'tay' – to this day I cannot pronounce upon that with any measure of certainty – but, as they sat there before me, I know that beyond all shadow of doubt I saw them become transformed, their splendour now so dazzling and variegated it was as if Gauguin the master were himself somehow present, bearing those wonders with him from his Tahitian Eden. Marvels destined for my eyes alone. And how I gazed upon them, magically lit now by the angled shafts of clear sunlight that criss-crossed the mock-terrazzo floor of the restaurant, squatting before me now in their rainbow-hued magnificence, what I can only describe as my Birds of Paradise.

Thenceforward, rarely a day passed but I winged with those exotic creatures across the Elysian Fields of my soul.

I was swaying hypnotically in that netherworld of the imagination, partaking of a brimful cup of sugared Brooke Bond, when what seemed as nothing so much as the passing of an unseen spectre awoke me and I looked up in horror to see Dingo Deery huddled deep in conversation with my pulchritudinous fledgelings, their wings folded over as if in protection or a prelude to his spiriting away. How my dream was shattered by the sight of his monochromatic amplitude! Through the crevasse of my fingers, I could discern his tiny eyes, phosphorescent with deceit, and in that instant I watched with a growing sense of unease as he drew the sleeve of the painter's overall across his mouth in a manner that banished the Tahitian genius, perhaps, I considered, never to return!

I fled, despondent, and walked the desolate streets. I felt as if something precious had died on me. I gave myself to Bacchus and that night slept beneath the open skies.

*

It is dificult, even to this day, to say when exactly things began to go wrong between my beloved uncle and me. Perhaps it was the fact that after my hasty departure from the café, he was forced to hire a horse and cart in order to locate me whilst I hopelessly fell from tavern to tavern, tormented by the valediction of my plumed beauties, put to flight by the accursed Deery!

His first words to me that fateful night as he came upon me in the open field where I lay beneath the stars were palpably devoid of the affectionate feeling which I had come to expect in my dealings with him, and we made our journey homeward in silence. There can be no doubt that shortly after this incident, a certain note of sourness became detectable in our relations.

This, however, was just the beginning. Within days, events had taken an even more serious turn. Uncle began to disappear for long periods, without so much as a word of explanation. The only indication that he had returned at all would be the gentle closing of the drawing-room door, the soft click to which my ears became accustomed as I lay there in the night waiting for the first light of dawn to touch the window. His absences grew increasingly more frequent until, as I stood by my bedroom window watching the silver dawn rise up over the rooftops, I clenched my fist in the pocket of my purple quilted dressing gown and at last confronted the fact which I could no longer deny: there was nothing for it but to investigate and discover once and for all the mysterious genesis of Uncle Louis's burgeoning eccentricities and the cause of his bewilderingly inexplicable nocturnal peregrinations. There was no longer any doubt in my mind that his animosity toward me was deepening by the day. I trawled my tormented conscience. Surely a single incident of boorish behaviour on my part could not have provoked such a bitter volte-face? Was there something else I had forgotten? Some vile act I had committed unknown to myself whilst in the grip of the demon grape? A murder, perhaps?

I paled. I wrung my hands in desperation as the grey-coated inspector of my mind paced the floor once more, investigating with rigorous, indeed fevered application. But it was all to no avail. The entropy of the vocative served only to confuse me further and the nets of my interrogations were returned, sadly empty once more.

However, as luck would have it, a certain pattern began to emerge. It gradually became clear that my relative's by now seething misanthropy was not directed solely at me. It had begun to extend to almost every citizen in the town.

It was after what I, for the purposes of narrative, shall call 'the telephone incident' that I realized that I could no longer indulge in my procrastinations and that any further dalliance on my part would undoubtedly be construed by future generations as moral cowardice. I had been standing for some time with my ear pressed to the oaken door of the library when, in odd, strangely muted tones, I heard him utter the words, 'So you think I'm at your beck and call, Mrs, do you?' followed by the ringing crash of the Bakelite receiver as it was slammed into its cradle and I heard him bellow: 'No! I won't be available for ornithology lectures! Tonight or any other fecking night! So put that in your drum and bang it!'

The muffled, indecipherable mutterings which followed seemed to cloak the entire building in a Satanic bleakness.

It was clear that I could delay no longer and I determined at once to unscramble as best I could this maddening conundrum, this ravelled web of perplexity that enshrouded my dear relative's life. That very night I began my vigil in the doorway of the tobacconist's shop which was situated directly across the road from the house. For three successive nights I remained at my post, and there were many occasions when I was tempted to swoon into the luxurious, beckoning arms of hopelessness. At last, however, on the fourth night of my vigil, my patience was rewarded and I froze as the massive front door of the house slowly opened and out stepped my uncle into the first, hesitant light of dawn. Hesitantly he scanned the empty street and then, pulling the collar of his sports coat up around his neck, began to stride briskly into the morning with his binocular case slung over his shoulder.

It was only when he turned left at the old humpbacked bridge that I realized he was making for the woods outside the town.

At once the scales fell from my eyes and I felt myself shrink to no more than five or six inches in height. Silently, I upbraided myself. How could I have been so foolish! To think ill of my dearest uncle! In those moments it all became clear to me and I understood perfectly, implicitly, the reasons for his recent erratic behaviour. His late-night pursuits of his ornithological obsessions had exhausted his body to the point that he had become the victim of an almost Hydesian change in his personality. And, like Hyde of course, he was completely unaware of it. I determined at once to waste no more time. I would explain this to him. I would be brutally frank and honest. Such a decision caused me no concern whatsoever. I knew he would see reason. I knew now that within a matter of days he would be back to himself and between us, all would be blissful as before. In that moment of realization, I exulted.

I continued to pursue Uncle Louis until he arrived at that clearing in the woods which overlooks the valley, from whence, he had on many occasions reminded me, it was possible at any one time to command a view of over thirty indigenous species of birds.

At first I thought that perhaps my nightly vigils had eroded my resilience to the point where my own mental equilibrium was already affected. Then, through a process of what might be termed cerebral massage, I succeeded in persuading myself that because of the all-pervasive heat which we in the town had been experiencing of late, the ... hallucinations – for what else could one call them – were unavoidable.

Between my dalliance and my delusions, my fate was sealed.

*

'Stay right where you are!' a raucous voice snapped. There was no mistaking the lumbering rotundity.

The corner of Dingo Deery's mouth curled like a decadent comma of flesh. I gasped and fell backwards onto a spiky clump of bracken, my foot, without warning, sinking into the marshmallow softness of a freshly manufactured cow pat.

The binoculars fell from my uncle's grasp as a swish of leaves stifled his cry.

I endeavoured to launch myself into flight but it was already too late. I found my neck locked in a vice grip as a megaphone-wielding Macardle appeared from the undergrowth, flanked by two of his burly henchmen. I watched helplessly as he stubbed his cigar on a bed of pine needles with the sole of his white Italian shoe, then slowly approached me, smiling faintly, squeezing the flesh of my cheek as if inspecting a fattened beast in a squalid market. He turned from me with disdain.

'Not bad!' he snapped. 'He'll do!' before abruptly losing interest in me and stalking off barking, 'Action!' into his pathetic trumpet.

I had to avert my gaze, for I could no longer bear to look upon that gross pantomime of the perverse which was before me.

*

My Birds of Paradise, divested of all but the most insignificant articles of clothing, were howling with glee and rapture as they cavorted lasciviously on the flattened grass. The bunched fleshy fingers of Dingo Deery like so many pork sausages caught me just below the spine as he bellowed: 'Go on, then – look away, you hypocrite! Pretend you don't see it!' Saliva dripped from his tobacco-stained teeth as his mocking eyes bit into me. Then he turned to my cowed relative and snarled: 'Louis Lestrange the Peeping Tom. Maybe you could tell us a little bit about that, Master? How about a lesson on that – eh? Today, boys, we are doing peeping! Haw haw haw!'

His mirth was unbridled as he continued. 'Thought you could get away with it, didn't you? I've been watching you for weeks, spying on us with them binoculars of yours! O yes –

I've been watching you, Master Peeping Tom Lestrange, and now, my friend, you are going to pay! You're going to pay for what you did to these . . .' He paused as the colour drained from his face. 'These hands!' He raised his extremities and displayed for all to see the lesions and contusions which even after all these years had not healed, the legacy of so many mathematical and linguistic miscalculations in a chalkdusty schoolroom of the long ago. His head seemed to swell to twice its normal size as all the blood in his body coursed rapidly towards it, his hands hovering menacingly in front of my uncle's face like two blotched table tennis bats of flesh.

'I'm sorry,' croaked my uncle, 'if there's anything I can do to make it up to you, Dingo – please tell me!'

But it was too late for any of that. It was clear that no one could help us now.

We found ourselves bound and gagged and imprisoned in the back of a foul-smelling vehicle which, it instantly became evident to us, as we lay there back to back like a nightmarish set of ill-proportioned Siamese twins, had been used in the very recent past for the transportation of poultry.

'Keep them in there until they have manners knocked into them!' I heard Dingo snarl, and the fading jackboot stomp of his wellingtons was the last sound that came to my ears before I collapsed at last into a dead faint.

*

As the days passed, our only contact with the outside world was the thin sword of light which shone when the double doors swung open, and a foul-smelling bowl of near-gruel was shoved towards us, our only means of sustenance throughout our captivity. How long was it going to go on, that wretched cacophony of sound that assaulted our eardrums daily like so many aural poison darts as we sweated in the darkness of our murky dungeon? 'Oh my God!' we would hear them shriek in orgiastic delight. 'That's great! Keep doing that!' as Macardle's coarse sibilants exhorted those poor corrupted creatures to indulge themselves to the point of what I knew must be certain destruction. 'Come on, girls,' he would cry. 'Get stuck in! Put your backs into it!'

In my ears, the sound of bodily fluids intermingling was as the roar of some horrible Niagara.

How long we spent in our foul confinement I cannot say. When at last they came to their decision regarding our fate, we were bundled out into the harsh light of day to confront the despicable Macardle, now disporting himself in a white shirt emblazoned with the lurid rubric MAC. A grin flexed itself across his face as he flicked his cigar and stared into my eyes. 'Ever done any acting, boy?' he enquired. 'No,' I croaked, feeling the first faint blush coming to my cheeks, and it was then he raised his hand and slowly opened it to display the photograph of my Uncle Louis, in what has been described as *flagrante delicto*, helpless as he lay in their powdered arms, folded in the delicate wings of my beautiful Birds of Paradise.

'I wonder what the parish priest would make of this?' snickered Macardle as he secreted the photograph in the inside pocket of his brown leather jacket.

'No, please!' I cried. 'Don't send it to the parish priest! Anything but that!'

Macardle coughed and pared the nail of his index finger with his marbled pocket knife.

'And just what's in it for me if I don't?' he quizzed stonily, his beadlike eyes slowly rising to meet mine.

'I'll do anything you say,' I said then, resigning myself at last to my fate.

*

Subsequently, everything is a dream. The nightly agonies of conscience which I suffered I cannot even begin to chronicle here for it would be too painful. All I can remember are the sad, hurt eyes of my dear Uncle Louis as the oaken arms of Dingo Deery gripped him once more and hurled him forward with a snort of derision, and the schoolmaster sank once again beneath a flutter of wings and the flying feathers of what once were Gauguin's masterpieces. But etched most of all on my mind is the twisted, salacious expression on the face of Mick Macardle as he distributed a variety of crook-handled canes, purchased by him for a pittance in a London East End market, and with which, through the medium of his barking metal trumpet, he instructed the cast, with unmistakable lip-trembling glee, to: 'Bate him harder! Hit him again there, girls! Give him all you've got!'

I hid my eyes as the blows rained down on the reddening flesh of my beloved uncle, his elderly moons thrust skyward as they continued to yelp excitedly: 'This will teach you! You won't be spying on us again in a hurry, you filthy-minded old rascal! Take that!'

The days passed in a black delirium as we were subjected to indignity after indignity, each day another can of eight-millimetre film sealed and labelled, just as surely as was our fate. Tears come into my eyes as those words return once more, thumbed that day by Deery onto a glinting reel: THE SECRETS OF LOUIS LESTRANGE.

I cannot continue. Sometimes I think perhaps it was all a

dream – not unlike what they insisted (and continued to, the fools, as if they could possibly know!) were no more than my fevered reconstructions of foul goings-on in a decrepit Amsterdam lock-up, for that was indeed how it appeared when it had all ended: the cameras spirited away, the convent reopened, the single tourist gone from the hotel: nothing remaining but the flattened yellow grass and the soft contented chirp of the chaffinches. I began to think maybe there never had been a Dingo Deery, a Mick Macardle, a thin moustache?

Would that it were true! I shall never forget the sight of that narrow, mean mouth, the unmistakable smell of cigar smoke that enshrouded me as I felt his hand grip my shoulder. 'If you ever breathe a word of this,' he hissed into my ear, 'the bating Lestrange got will be nothing to what's coming to him!'

I thought of my uncle, his spirit now broken beyond repair, his white-swaddled hands for all the world the blunt stumps of a war veteran as he picked his way sheepishly through the cooling streets.

Oh yes, Mick Macardle and Dingo Deery existed all right, for in the few days that remained to me in the town, they missed no opportunity to humiliate me, whispering discreetly as they passed close by: 'I believe you're a powerful actor, young man!' and 'Did you ever try the stage?'

I began to dread these forced intimacies to such a degree that I became a virtual recluse.

The long hot summer came to an end. Grouse Armstrong met his death in an accident with a Volkswagen Beetle and the only sound to be heard now in the Pronto Grill was that of the proprietor whistling his lonely tune, dreaming of Palermo. Not long after, Mick Macardle opened a supermarket, the very first of its kind in the country, and ever since is to be seen cruising around brashly in his open-topped convertible in streets that are now littered with drug addicts and disco bars. I understand he has entered politics and resides in a magnificent converted castle on the outskirts of the town, with Dingo Deery resplendent in his blue security uniform by the electronically surveyed gates, his embrocated extremities now encased in gloves of the softest calf leather.

What bitter injustice there is in this world!

And now in this great city, as beneath my window the cinema doors open and the hunted, clandestine penumbrae emerge from the subterranean flesh-palace to shuffle homeward like so many tormented spectres, I realize at last that there is little for me to do but accept the hand that fate has dealt me. For, having hastily terminated my academic studies and fled the country all those years ago, who am I to complain of a lowly position with Brent Council? For in truth they have treated me most fairly and my supervisor has informed me that the section of Kilburn Park for which I am responsible is considered impeccable and utterly leaf-free and has been singled out for special mention by the visiting inspectors on more than three occasions.

Yes, the old men have long since passed away now, the Summer Seat taken away and broken up for firewood. To smoke a Player's cigarette now is to put oneself in great mortal danger and they say that since Yuri Gagarin returned from space he has become a complete vegetable. But I shall not rest. Deep inside my quest shall go on, my relentless search for refuge from those terrible memories and the wanton destruction of what was once a beautiful dream.

Which of course they shall never know. How would they, those sad, anonymous creatures who shuffle homeward to their waiting, unsuspecting wives, their base desires sated? How are they ever to know that what they have just witnessed on that oblong obscenity they call a screen is the vilest of lies, a distortion, a cruel, ugly trick played by a cheap magician? Would they listen to me if I were to cry out from the very pit of my soul: '*The Secrets of Louis Lestrange*! It is lies, my friends! Lies! This is all lies! A pack of despicable, unwarranted lies! Don't believe a word of it!'

No, in my heart I know they would not. So, I have no choice but to go on, with the memory of those days which were once suffused with the colour of burnished copper receding within me, nothing more now than a bit player from the last reel of the deserted cinema of life, where a silent, would-be ornithologist, once honoured and revered beyond all rustic pedagogues, sits alone in the back row, staring into the dust-clouded lenses of a pair of old binoculars, chuckling to himself without reason as he tries to focus on the past and the way it might have been, before a thin moustache, a cruel twist of fate and 1,137 whacks of a crook-handled cane brought an old man and a poor young adolescent boy to within eight lonely millimetres of hell.

The Luck of
Dympna Wrigley

Ever since she had been forced to give up her job in the civil service, Dympna Wrigley, aged thirty-five, of Immaculata Parade, Barntrosna, had been living with her mother and would have gladly killed her ('Who's goanta look after me! Who's goanta to look after me!') if she had the chance because she was driving her mad and had been ever since her husband's death. Sitting in the chimney corner with her stockings around her ankles like gravy rings, croaking about this and croaking about that and demanding to know what exactly it was she had done to deserve a daughter the like of Dympna. If she was a daughter at all, a cheeky, good-for-nothing lump more like, who never did so much as a hand's turn around the house. Who cared about nothing or no one and who, if her poor mother was to drop dead right there on the spot, probably wouldn't so much as shed a tear over her grave. Indeed would most likely be more than glad to get rid of her, for that was the kind of her, wasn't it, a lousy, rotten, miserable and ungrateful wretch not worthy of the name daughter. O no daughter, Mrs Nellie Wrigley had no daughter.

It was only to be expected that eventually an unsettling little smile found its way onto the face of Dympna Wrigley and she surprised herself by thinking:

—You know, Mama, if you keep on talking like that, I really do think I shall have to stab you with a knife!

She scraped some more muck off the plates and camou-flaged her chuckling by rattling the crockery in the sink as she thought of herself standing over the spindly old dwarf – for what else was she! – with the knife, going:

—What's that you say, Mama? What am I doing with the knife, Mama? Why, I'm going to kill you with it, of course!

But if it was going to be great fun killing her, thought Dympna, it would be even more exciting burying her. 'Good-bye, old scarecrow! Ta ta!' she would cry triumphantly. 'Off to the worms!'

There would, of course, be no need for a coffin. She'd simply toss her in in her baglady's rags. That would be good enough for her, wouldn't it? But of course! Then – at last! – over her dead and buried body, to be able to read: *Here lies Old Nellie Wrigley. In life she was a wizened old cow and in death she's even worse! But at least, thank God, she's quiet!*

—What are you doing out there? demanded the scrakey voice from within.

—I'm just doing the dishes, Mama! replied Dympna as a spark of flinty fire leaped in her eyes, and she clenched her suds-mottled fists with resolve.

*

For she knew she would not be doing the dishes for very much longer. What she could not for the life of her understand was how it had taken her so long to come up with a plan. As she dried her hands, she just could not believe how she had tolerated the litter-strewn abscess that called itself a village, for so long weeping at night in a kitchen that smelt of chickens without ever once taking a defiant stand and saying to herself:

—I'm getting out of this dump! To hell with her, the

whingeing old crone! And to hell with Barntrosna! You hear me – to hell with you!

Which was what she was most definitely saying now – O, but yes! At the very same time as she was emptying some fine white powder from a broken capsule into Mama Scaldcrow's soothing evening drink!

—Is my drink ready yet, you? snapped the voice with the timbre of a rusty swinging gate.

—Oh yes, Mama! Oh but yes, my repugnant scarecrow mother!

The last part Dympna didn't say, of course. Simply let it pass across her mind. But ensured that she did not in any way permit it to interfere with the heart-warming smile with which she greeted Señorita Hag as she handed her the steaming cup of hot cocoa to help her with her night-time sleep. Which it would certainly do and no mistake – Hag need have no fear of that! Why, with a bit of luck, she wouldn't wake up for at least a month! By which time, Dympna would be far away, waltzing through the streets of Dublin City, with her life and all the world before her. With handsome men coming up to her and saying:

—I want you to be my wife – come and live with me for ever!

Already, her vanity case was packed and ready for the road, and thrown hastily across it the only garment Dympna Wrigley possessed that even vaguely resembled an overcoat. Which, in fact, looked like any number of rats sewn clumsily together. But that too would very soon change. Inevitably, Dympna Wrigley knew, when her fortunes changed, when about her shoulders there would be draped the most expensive furs that money could buy, and upon her pale white arms more jewellery than you would hear rattling in the whole of Hollywood.

A ripple of excitement was running through her body as she thought of all that was yet to be, when just then she heard the muffled piggy snores coming from the direction of the chimney corner. In that instant, the state of ecstasy in which Dympna Wrigley found herself became almost unbearable. Particularly when she gingerly tiptoed towards the kitchen door and with one eye peeped in to establish the state of the wheezing assemblage of badly baked turnover loaves who called herself Mother. And who – to her absolute delight! – was – if not lying there with a large breadknife inserted in her chest – was at least, to all intents and purposes, completely dead to the world! Which meant that for Dympna Wrigley – once and for all! – it was time to put into action the second part of her plan!

Within seconds she had her ticket purchased and the train was speeding towards Dublin like a firework shooting into the night.

And as Dympna Wrigley sat alone there in her carriage – a little tense, it must be admitted, for the furthest she had ever been from Barntrosna was to the neighbouring village of Killyhoe to visit her Uncle Dan – behind her eyes a thousand tiny worlds of possibility glittered, each one about to expand in all directions into a phantasmagoric universe all of its own. As the former civil servant pulled her rat-coat about her, she gave a little shiver, consoling herself with the knowledge that soon it would be the finest mink or sable, and that the streets of Dublin would grind to a halt, stunned into silence as she swept by, then crying:

—My God! It's Dympna! Dympna Wrigley!

*

Her first experiences were truly glorious, there can be no denying it; with the few shillings she had in her possession, Dympna Wrigley ensured that she had the time of her life! 'If I eat another ice-cream cone,' she exclaimed excitedly to the sympathetic counter assistant in Forte's Grill in O'Connell Street, 'I shall surely go up like a balloon! I wonder what millionaire playboy will want me then?'

Yes, initially, there can be no doubt, Dympna found herself living in a kind of Paradise in Dublin City. But, within days, certain ominous shadows had begun to encircle her and the reasonably attractive woman in her mid-thirties whose optimism knew no bounds found herself sitting by the window in a dingy café staring out at the emptying streets, the first pangs of guilt beginning to claw at her, small voices subtly insinuating themselves as they whispered:

—So this is what it was all for, Miss Dympna Wrigley? This is why you left your poor mother? You know that she might be dead, don't you? You know your poor mother who washed and clothed and fed you might be dead! She might be dead, Dympna Wrigley! Dead! Dead! Dead!'

It was only a matter of time before they breached her defences, these marshalled front-line troops of undiluted guilt, and finally she placed both her clenched fists against her eyes and began to sob. 'Why oh why did I have to go and do it, leave my happy home to come to this awful place where nobody gives a damn whether I live or die? How could you have been so stupid, Dympna Wrigley! How?' she chided herself.

After that, she took to walking through the streets with reddened eyes, somewhere close by a reedy organ plaintively piping as she stood staring into shop windows with all their beautiful finery and jewellery. What was it the song seemed to say to her as a silver tear dried in the corner of her eye?

I am a young girl wandering.
Dympna, Dympna Wrigley is my name;
Wandering without hope, without purpose,
When will I find love?

A question to which, as time progressed, there did not appear to be an answer. Certainly none that Dympna Wrigley could elucidate, at any rate, as now, like some broken doll, she found herself sitting on the edge of a fountain with her bag in her hand and the waters crashing behind her as she groaned pitifully:

—I am a bad woman. I am a stupid woman and a bad woman to do what I have done. To leave my poor mama alone to die.

As her tendency towards self-laceration grew, her self-confidence began to evaporate in almost equal measure. In fact her confidence now seemed nothing more than a pathetic contrivance in the face of the ragged, predatory figures who surrounded her as they remorselessly attempted to wrest her handbag and its sad few contents from her grasp. 'Oi! Miss! Got any odds? Giv's a few quid!' they would harshly call from street corners, secure behind their wet-tipped cigarettes, Dympna's flat heels clattering onward in a night air shattered by the sound of coarse and cold-blooded laughter.

All of which might not have overwhelmed her had it not been for the added anxieties induced by the relentless clamour, the forlorn cries that criss-crossed the night as though the heart-rending pleas of faceless pariahs in some bottomless void, the sudden clang of pinball machines and the swirling phantas-magoria of lights and music which rendered her helpless with a feeling of sickly dizziness and provoked in her a desire for only one thing – to be back in the tranquil haven of her home village – the place she had so stupidly, callously turned her back on!

And to which she was within days of returning – until that fateful night when her life was irrevocably changed for ever.

—It'll be all right, honeybun! Dermo said to her, extending his hand as he smiled at her across the formica expanse of the corner table in the San Remo Café (despite her tears, she managed to discern the words LOVE and MUM etched upon the brown limb in spidery letters of startling blue) and, with twinkling, magnanimous eyes enquiring as to whether perhaps she might accompany him to his place of residence for a cup of hot soup – that it might make her feel better?

How fortune could have seen fit to smile on her in such a compassionate, yielding manner, Dympna Wrigley could not understand, and as she took Dermo's arm, now accompanying him through the glittering streets of night (in which she all of a sudden felt herself so utterly comfortable and 'at home' that it actually astonished her) she was so happy, in fact, she felt like addressing the entire city of Dublin! Felt like crying out: 'At last! At last! Dympna Wrigley is happy!' For the simple reason that she wanted everyone to know! Know that she, Dympna – who had once been the most miserable girl in all of Dublin City – was now as close to bursting with contentment as she had ever been, or hoped to be!

But might have been a little more circumspect if she had but known just what sort of a character she had now permitted herself to stroll alongside in the suspiciously benign city streets! And perhaps might not – if she'd left the village of Barntrosna at least once in her life before having encountered him – have so readily placed her trust in Dermo Slattery. Would, most certainly, have given it a lot more thought when he said:

—Don't worry, honeybun! I'm the man'll look after you!, instead of blurting out:

—Oh thank you, Dermo! Thank you ever so much!, right there and then and plunging herself into what was about to become a nightmare with someone who – even if only because of his slender moustache and the absurd cornucopia of gold rings upon his fingers – ought to have excited at the very least a soupçon of suspicion. Not that she would have been expected to cry:

—Oh no! I know your lot! A pimp! I can smell them a mile away!

Of course not. But she would, without doubt, have approached her situation with a little more wariness. Instead of trotting back to his flat with a great big smile on her face, innocently climbing into bed with him and slavishly following his instructions until they were both, as they might have quaintly described it in Barntrosna, 'at it hammer and tongs', like they'd known one another all their lives. Central to this, of course, was Dermo's insistence that she was the most beautiful girl he had ever seen in his life. This, perhaps because she heard it so rarely – never before, in fact – proved such a source of delight to Dympna that presently she was insisting to her new-found companion that she would be honoured to do anything for him. 'And I mean – *anything*!' she cried shrilly, her body happily contorting into the shape of a crab as her head tapped out a somewhat primitive musical rhythm on the flock wallpaper.

A statement which, as it turned out, proved to be a lot truer than she thought, for within a matter of days – to her perplexity – she was to be found standing outside the railway station, generously elevating her hemline and offering to accompany men – complete strangers – back to Dermo's place for a 'cup of tea'.

How exactly he had managed to secure her agreement continued to remain something of a mystery to her – perhaps he had drugged her? – but within a matter of a few paltry weeks it was as though she'd been standing by the ornamental fountain which was located outside the main city railway station for most of her adult life.

It was only a matter of time, of course, and sure enough, within a few short months, all her old nightmares had returned with a vengeance and it was not uncommon to see her sitting on the concrete surround of the fountain with her elbows on her knees as her cheap mascara (insisted upon by Dermo) intermingled with the tears which now cascaded hopelessly down her cheeks. Now, however, her 'new-found friend' did not prove to be quite so understanding. Informing her, in fact, that if she didn't quit her crying 'double quick' and 'get down to that railway station' as 'fast as her knobbly pins' would take her, that she'd be the sorry girl and just to prove his point shoved his ring-bedecked fist into her face. And so, each day, it was off once more to offer her body (at ludicrously low prices – 'Turnover! Turnover!' Dermo would shriek when she protested) to the streams of train-travelling, shifty-eyed men, and endure anew the guilt she prayed had vanished for ever.

But which most certainly had not – in fact was if anything worse than before because on top of the crime she had perpetrated on her ailing mother she was now faced with the enormity of her sins against holy purity. All of which ended up with her pacing the evening streets once more, a crumpled mass of tears and cheap satin clothing, the reedy organ again piping its melancholy tune as she stood longingly in front of plate-glass windows bedecked with flowers, cards and the tiny tokens that lovers exchange.

> *I am a young girl wandering*
> *Searching through these city streets*
> *For the love I hoped to find*
> *I don't think I'll ever find it*

Dympna Wrigley sniffed to herself that the likes of Dermo was all that she deserved. Especially after the way she'd behaved. 'How could I do it on my own flesh and blood?' she howled as she pummelled the glass in the warm, heartbroken night.

In the end, she became a shadow of her former self, threshing about under anonymous mounds of primeval, perspiring flesh until she had long since lost count, always close by the shadow of Dermo counting his ill-gotten gains. Continuing to insist to her: 'I love you, my honeybun!'

Lies, of course! she thought as a seventeen-stone man reached for his trousers. Just another instance of Dermo Slattery and his tawdry lies!

Not that she cared any more – she was well beyond that. Or seemed to be, at any rate! Until fate once more took a hand and the path of Dympna Wrigley crossed with that of – it is impossible! Such things happen only in fiction! – one of the city's most prominent and celebrated citizens, *Dr Kiernan McSwiggan*! An extraordinary stroke of good fortune, for not only was Dr McSwiggan one of Dublin's most renowned art buyers and all-round cultured gentlemen, he was also a millionaire many times over and lived in a castle on the outskirts of the city!

When she first heard the words passing his lips, it was all Dympna Wrigley could do not to spit in the face of this so-called 'refined epicurean'. For the sentence 'I love you' meant as much to her now as the tail of a sewer rat. Which was why, in that instant, she turned from him, once more thrusting her clenched fist into her mouth, the red-faced bon viveur proceeding contentedly, rhythmically above her.

But in the days that followed it occurred to Dympna Wrigley that there had been something about the fine-art connoisseur and the way he had uttered those words — for so long in the mouths of others indisputably hollow — and actually on repeated visits continued to *insist* upon repeating, *I love you! I love you! I love you! O Dimpy I love you!*, and always giving her that special look as he did so, that soon she began to soften ever so slightly and reveal her innermost thoughts to him — confidences she had never imparted to anyone! Concerning her mother and the little village where she was born and the many dreams which had so heartbreakingly turned to dust when she came to horrible, horrible Dublin. But most of all, regarding Dermo and the terrible things he had done to her, imprisoning her in bamboo cages and making her dress up in rabbit costumes.

The latter part was essentially embellishment but the instant he heard these words spoken, the change that overcame the normally mild-mannered McSwiggan was quite shocking in its impact. Pounding the wall with his fist, he swore — Dympna feared a cardiac arrest — that if this 'Dermo' — this 'wretched louse from the armpit of the earth' — ever so much as laid another finger on her she was to proceed without delay to his castle and inform him.

Which was all very well, of course, except for the fact that when Dermo realized that 'that shitebag McSwiggan' as he derisively called him — Dermo despised culture in all its forms — was attracted to his 'honey', as he put it, not only did he lay a finger on her, he punched her so hard that she went flying across the room and knocked her head forcefully against the fridge, with the result that the next day her eye had swollen up the size of a shining blood-gorged cockroach.

From the moment – the very second – the Modigliani authority (for he was such) set eyes upon that hideous iris, the die was already cast. Dermo, of course, pronounced himself not 'the slightest bit afraid' of 'Bollocky-Balls McSwiggan', for, he continued, he was nothing more than a 'useless big hoor with a fat cigar' and not worth giving so much as a second thought to. Which, as far as the well-known gourmet (his taste and experience were legendary throughout the city) was concerned, might have been true but most definitely was not when it came to his two muscular bodyguards, who, as a consequence of the plentiful wages paid to them each week (not to mention innumerable 'tokens' and regular 'somethings for themselves'), would have done absolutely anything required of them by 'the Doc', as they genially called him.

Which Dermo was about to find out, as he was on his way home from the video shop, with a copy of – ironically! – *The Kidnapping* tucked neatly under his arm, whistling innocently, when he found the ground giving way beneath him, and the sound of squealing brakes, seeming far away now when in fact the stretch limousine was speeding towards the deserted factory where he was to find himself beaten to a pulp and warned that if he ever approached Dympna Wrigley again what he had just received would be as nothing. 'Nothing? You hear?' they snapped at him, as the still-warm cosh was slipped snugly and receptively into a back pocket. 'Yes,' croaked Dermo, raising a tattered and obsequious hand, 'please . . . I beg you! No more!'

After that, Dympna's life changed dramatically. Now,

instead of rambling wet-eyed through the night-time streets pursued by the heartlessly persistent laments of reedy organs, casting her eyes longingly over beautiful silks and satins she knew she would never own, wondering where it was love might be found, she was being driven everywhere in a stretch limousine almost as big as the street she had been born in, with Kiernan showering presents on her and pecking her on the cheek and telling her she was the most beautiful woman he had ever set eyes on and how every day he thanked God for 'sending him his little angel from heaven'. Before, finally, eventually, slipping to his knees to ask her to marry him. A request which, reluctantly, she had to turn down with the words: 'I'm sorry, Kiernan. But I have evaded my responsibilities for long enough. I must go! Back to Barntrosna where my ageing, abandoned mother awaits!'

Of course she did, which is why three days later the bells were ringing out over Dublin City and a radiant Mrs Dympna McSwiggan was standing in the doorway of a cathedral showered in paper bells and horseshoes, endeavouring without success to stifle her giggles as her new husband kissed her yet again, the boisterous cacophony of tin cans and old boots following them all the way to the airport.

Sometimes, adrift on her lilo in the months that followed, Dympna would fancy she could hear familiar squawks that were not unlike those which had been known to emanate from a certain chimney corner in what was now the long ago. But beneath the hot, burning sun of Tuscany it was impossible to say.

As it was to be certain that the weasly, slender-moustached visage which occasionally formed itself on the blue wobbling water belonged to that of a man she had once known as

Dermo Slattery. Which was why Dympna simply put these occurrences down to the heat, and, draping a towel about her bronzed and slender frame, would chuckle softly as she strolled across the terrazza towards the villa and into the outstretched arms of her cigar-chomping, wolf-grinning husband.

The Big Prize

Pats Donaghy had always harboured notions of becoming a world-famous writer but to say that he found himself speechless and utterly flummoxed when it actually happened would be what you might call the understatement of the century. It all began one Saturday some three years ago now when he was coming down the stairs. A letter lying in the hallway caught his eye. His first inclination was to ignore it completely and go on about his business and have his breakfast. But something drew him back. He hesitated for a moment and then began his journey towards the mysterious white rectangle of paper. It bore none of the hallmarks of the customary missives cursorily dispatched to him by the likes of *Reader's Digest* and Quality Book Club. Disdainfully, he tore it open. 'Gasp!' he exclaimed. 'It's about my novel!' And so it was. His latest work, on which he had been labouring for almost two years – *A Kalashnikov for Shamus Doyle* – had scooped the Buglass-McKenzie Literary Prize!

'What madness is this?' he asked himself. 'Pats Donaghy, are you in your right mind at all? Who with any wit is going to give you all that money for a bit of a book?'

He feared that all those nights wrestling with the formless shadows of his fevered imagination had finally taken their toll.

He went inside and bit his nail as his mammy poured him a cup of tea. He resolved to make no reference whatsoever to his momentary delusion in case she might say:

—Will you stop this nonsense now, Pats, or you'll get what's coming to you!

But just then the door burst open and his sister Nabla burst in.

—Mammy! Mammy! Did you hear the news? she declared hoarsely. Pats has won a big prize in England!

She threw her arms around her brother and cried:

—I'm proud of you, Pats Donaghy!

Pats reddened a little and lowered his head.

—Would you look at the cut of me! his mammy cried out. I can't go to England like this!

But that night in bed she said that she was proud of him. She tickled his ear and whispered:

—Maybe one day you'll write a little book about me, will you, Pats?

—Oh, Mammy, Pats said and she laughed and he laughed and then all he could remember was Mammy in his dream coming charging down Charing Cross Road with all her Fenwick's bags shouting:

—Yoo hoo! Wait for me, Pats!

*

At last the big day came and they were off to London. Shoots McGilly with the one eye drove them to the station. He said he had met plenty of English people and in his opinion there was nothing wrong with them. Nabla said:

—Oh, Pats! I think I'm going to have a fit in this aeroplane!

But she didn't. Didn't it turn out she knew one of the hostesses – a Maureen Fletcher from Blessed Martin de Porres Avenue.

—God, isn't it gas! exclaimed Maureen with her hands on her hips. The places you meet people!

—I'd say there'll be a big crowd in London tonight, mused Nabla, and Maureen agreed.

—There will indeed, Nabla, she said.

Meanwhile Pats and Mammy went on chatting away about all the things they were going to buy in London. She told him she had always known he was going to be a famous writer ever since the time he got nine out of ten for his composition 'Gathering Blackberries'. (*The Angelus Bell was ringing as we came over the hill, our faces smeared in purple blackberry juice and our billy cans glinting in the sun.*)

—Laws! cried Pats. When I think of it!

—I was always proud of you, son, she said, but I won't rest until you write a little book about me.

—Don't worry, Mammy, Pats promised, and she gave a little wiggle, I will.

And would you believe it – ten minutes later they had landed in Heathrow!

*

Mammy and Pats were in room 245 and Nabla had a room to herself on the second floor. Pats hadn't been so excited since the day of his first communion. Outside, the lights of Shaftesbury Avenue winked at him and said: 'Wotcher, Pats – you're in the dosh now, ain'tcha?'

And it was true, wasn't it? All thanks to two people – Mammy and Shamus Doyle.

What was it the *Times Literary Supplement* had said about him?

The modern Irish novel is in safe hands at last – take a bow, Mr Donaghy!

They had even printed a little piece of his humble effort. It was the part where Shamus vows to Cait that he will never kill again.

Cait tossed back her flame-haired locks angrily and spun away from him.

—Oh you! she snapped, and he went to her, gripping her by the shoulders.

—You don't understand, he cried, you'll never understand, Cait Maguire!

She winced.

—I do understand. I understand more than you'll ever know, Shamus Doyle! I understand that there were twenty-two small schoolchildren on that bus! Twenty-two little boys and girls who never stood a chance!

Doyle lit a cigarette with trembling hands.

—I told you that was a mistake! he hissed.

—She spat contemptuously.

—A mistake? Is that what you call it? You have a nerve calling yourself a human being, Shamus Doyle!

It goes on and on like that and then in the end Shamus says:

—I promise I won't kill any more people, Cait.

And she says:

—Oh, Shamus!

Meanwhile, however, his old friend One-Shot Danny McClatchey has been dispatched by the organization to see that he is terminated with extreme prejudice – but listen! What am I talking about! thought Pats as he munched the duvet.

*

—*And now – the winner of this year's Buglass-McKenzie Prize, Mr Pats Donaghy!*

Pats was as nervous as a kitten, making his speech. He kept thinking of the whole town in front of their tellies going:

—Would you look at Donaghy! Just who does he think he is!

So he made sure to thank everybody in the town and especially Shoots McGilly for driving them to the station. He said it was wonderful to be in London: 'The city that never sleeps!' he said. 'And I can assure you I didn't sleep last night – ha ha!' he laughed.

He went on to talk about Madame Tussaud's and how much his mammy had liked being in Selfridge's and John Lewis and all the places they had been that day. And he especially thanked the sponsors Buglass-McKenzie for making it all possible. When he said that, they all began to clap, and one of the critics took over and said that Pats' writing was at the cutting edge of the new Irish urban realism. He said that *A Kalashnikov for Shamus Doyle* was a bullet up the backside of literary complacency. When she heard that, Mammy said,

—The language of him, Pats!, but she was only joking.

Then they had lots of wine to drink and they met a man and a woman who said:

—Will you say awfter again for us, please.

So they did. They said:

—After we leave here, we're going back to the hotel.

They thought this was a great laugh altogether and said:

—Have some more wine.

—Aaahfter! they kept saying, but they couldn't say it as good as Pats and Mammy and Nabla.

Then it was a taxi and home to bed for everyone. Mammy

was wearing a nightdress she had bought in Janet Reger's. She said,

—I must look a sight, but Pats said,

—You do not, Mammy, you look radiant.

—Oh Pats, she said, and Pats said:

—Mammy, do you know what I'm going to do with the money, I'm going to bring you on a world cruise. She said,

—And Nabla as well? But Pats said:

—No, Mammy, just you.

Little did he know at that time just how true those fateful words were to prove, for hardly had they gone two miles in Shoots' hackney car after he had picked them up at Dublin airport ('There youse are!' he had cried with a wide sweep of his cap) when a flock of sheep appeared out of nowhere and swept straight across the road.

—Look out! cried Shoots as he spun the wheel. There was a sickening thud and when he came round Pats saw that Nabla was dead.

—Mammy! he cried out.

—Pats! Is that you? she replied.

—Yes, Mammy, it is! he wept, relieved.

The sad part about that accident was that Shoots was killed too.

*

After that, the grief was too much for them to bear. Everywhere they went about the house, they were confronted with memories of Nabla: her forget-me-not pinafore, the holy pictures and her pink squashy house slippers. Despite repeated cancellations, her copy of *Woman's Way* continued to arrive like some persecution from beyond the grave. In the end it all became too much for both of them so they sold up everything they owned and moved away from the town.

*

They found Dublin City very much to their liking – except perhaps for the smelly O'Hare family, who became their first neighbours when they lived in temporary rented accommodation on the Miami Towers Estate. There were fourteen of them and four pit-bull terriers – Norman Bates, Pancho, Elvis and Dirty Den. Mr O'Hare worked in the local crisp factory but had been made redundant and turned to selling wellington boots from a stall by the side of the dual carriageway. As he said himself:

—Booted out and sellin' boots!

Noeleen was the young girl of the family, and a very pretty young lady she was too, if a trifle curt in manner, as Pats discovered one day on his way home from Waterstone's with a copy of the *London Review of Books*. He stopped for a moment to chat to her about school and the approaching exams, only to be taken aback when she said:

—Never mind about school – do you want a jump or not?

He demurred and hastened on his way.

Then there was Nialler, who stole cars and raced them up and down the dual carriageway. He had quite a selection in his front garden. Rarely a day passed but he greeted Pats in the traditional manner of the estate:

—Howya, Bukes! I'll buke your bleedin' bollix in!

It was just as well none of them could read, Pats would often reflect. He shuddered to think what their reaction might have been if they'd found out just what he'd been up to all those nights with his ear to the wall while they were having their

119

colourful, expletive-speckled family debates; especially when Noeleen got in the family way and it turned out to be Nialler's! There certainly was a lot of consternation in the abode of the O'Hares that evening! It took Mr O'Hare almost two hours to bear the truth out of the miscreant with the Krooklok.

—Didja?

—Wha?

—You know wha!

—Did I wha', Da?

—Don't fukkin' didja wha' me!

It got so bad that Mrs O'Hare could bear it no longer and began to fling the remnants of the evening meal – half-eaten batter burgers and sodden chips – at the man she had married in St Anne's Church, Raheny, twenty-two years before.

—Leave him alone, Da! she snapped, as another salvo whistled past his ear. He wiped the ketchup off his chin with an expansive sweep of his forearm and snarled back at her.

—Don't hurt the girl, Jim, for the love and honour of St Joseph!

Mr O'Hare landed a punch in the middle of his daughter's forehead and faced his wife defiantly.

—DON'T FUKKIN' TELL ME WHAT TO DO! JA HEAR ME, RIGH'?

But happily it was all resolved in the end, with the contrite Nialler being dispatched to the Italia Bar for a dozen stout and some drugs for himself and Noeleen. And, as the singing and dancing started – 'Here we go! Here we go! Here we go!' and 'Olé! Olé! Olé!' the head of the household was heard to gaily whoop atop the gas cooker – the unfortunate pregnancy was all but forgotten. As Mrs O'Hare put it, after a nip or two of sherry:

—I don't care if the little fucker has four eyes – he's still an O'Hare, righ', Nialler?

And Nialler said:

—Righ', Ma! as Elvis, Norman Bates, Pancho and Dirty Den sang background vocals to Mr O'Hare's impromptu Pavarotti.

*

Unfortunately, Mammy and Pats never did get to see the baby as they were notified shortly afterwards that the building work had all been completed and they were free to move into their new sixteen-bedroomed property overlooking the sea in the salubrious suburb of Dalkey in south Dublin. But the story of the wonderful O'Hare family was far from over . . .

For yes – you've guessed!

The notification came as before, in a plain white vellum envelope, and it simply stated that Pats' novel *Back of a Lorry* – about the trials and tribulations of an ordinary Dublin family – had scooped the Buglass-McKenzie Prize once more. Had things been otherwise, he would have raced back upstairs and cried:

—Mammy! I did it! I won again!

But sadly, not long after they moved into their new home, his mammy began to suffer from pre-senile dementia, and nothing would sway her from the conviction that not only was Pats not her son but that he was, in fact, His Eminence Pope John Paul, the head of the one true Church.

But that is all in the past. It matters little to Pats Donaghy now that the critics champion *A Kalashnikov for Shamus Doyle* and *Back of a Lorry* as masterpieces of our time. He is only too aware that it is not a writer's job to pass comment on his own work. His obligation is to simply carry on and do what it is he was put on this earth to do.

Literary prizegivings are of little consequence to him.

And if perchance his new novel does catch the critical imagination and he finds himself once more gazing upon the variegated splendour of that most wondrous of cities, he will most certainly accept them graciously. But until then there are many exotic and beguiling lands to visit, the world opening like a dazzling oyster before himself and Mammy as they board the vessel which is to take them far from their native shores, to the white, powdered sands of the South Sea Islands, where beneath waving palms on a wickerwork table he shall forge ahead with his latest opus, *The Barntrosna Files*, in which a shy young man is confronted by a series of events which eventually make him face the truth about himself. A work which may well indeed see him take his place once more, nut brown and monkey-suited, upon that august podium, to make his speech. A night which shall be his crowning glory, for he will have kept his promise to Mammy so many years ago, and all those little tiddles will not have been in vain. But that is all to come, and there is much mango fruit and coconut milk to be consumed between now and then. His typewriter keys clack as baby monkeys shriek and chatter happily as Mammy's laughter floats on the balmy breeze as she sips mint juleps and arranges audiences with him for favoured villagers. Pats strikes each key singly, meticulously:

> It was morning in Barntrosna. Or should I say evening. There was rain forecast. 'I see there's rain forecast,' said Mickey Niblett's mother as she wound the skein of blue wool around her stiff, almost waxen hands that were pointed outwards as if she were pretending she had just caught a large fish, such as a trout. Just then there was a

knock at the door. Mickey got up from his chair and smiled as he raised his hand and said: 'No, Mammy – I'll get it.' He had a little difficulty with the front door latch because it was a trifle stiff. But there was no need to worry because Daddy had promised to attend to it when he got home from the fair. At last the door swung open and, to his horror, Mickey found himself shot three times through the head with a .357 Magnum, which is the most powerful handgun in the world. Had he not been wearing his lead-insulated protective helmet, he almost certainly would have died. 'Phew! That was a close one, Mammy, wasn't it?' he said, wiping his perspiring brow. 'Come here to me, Mickey Niblett, and never mind them would-be assailants or whoever it is they are! Do you hear me? Come away on over here now and give me a kiss, lovey,' she cried, 'for you're the best wee writer in the whole of Barntrosna town!'

The Boils of Thomas Gully

Tom Gully is a farmer from Cloonee, which is a small townland approximately one mile from the village of Barntrosna. Tom is a very nice man but he is not really what you would call the very attractive film-star type. Which he wishes he were but he knows that it is impossible and has long since resigned himself to the situation. As he says himself: 'Sure, if I have a few pounds in my pocket and have the couple of pints at night, what's the use in complaining?' He is a creature of habit, Tom. Being a farmer, every morning he drives his tractor into the village to leave his milk churns to be collected. Then he goes to the post office to lodge a few shillings into his account and after that it's into Shamey Henley's for one or two glasses of stout. That's all, mind, for there are always plenty of chores to be done in the afternoon – groceries, fertilizer to be purchased, boots to be left into the shoemakers and so on. Then it's off down the high road for Cloonee once again, with you motoring along in your stuttering old tractor. But at least with a nice warm glow about your person that you didn't have when you came in. And which you'd need, if your name was Tom Gully, at any rate, because when Tom arrives home and goes inside to his rickety old farmhouse, the very same sentence always falls from his lips: 'What kind of an eejit am I that I can't get myself a woman? Everybody else has one!' Which was not entirely true but there would be no point in disputing it with Tom. It would only end with him slumping into the armchair with his head in his hands, self-consciously tweaking at the boil which had emerged on his forehead at the age of thirty-two, sighing that no matter what you said he hadn't a woman and that was all that mattered. And not much sign of getting one either. O, there had been times all right when it looked as if his prayers were about to be answered – particularly when the young Cooney one from Longfield Cross had agreed to allow him drive her home – even kiss her indeed! But in the end it had all come to nothing and she had married a McGarry from Kilkeerin and was never seen again. There had been another girl too, a Teresa McMenamin who had the most beautiful hair that Tom Gully had ever seen. Hair so soft and clean and fine that it made him want to almost die, such was the feeling of coarseness and crudity it provoked within him as regards the nature of his own rotund and somewhat unkempt physical aspect. A feeling which he went on to experience on many, many occasions, before Teresa finally announced that she was moving to the city of Dublin to further her nursing career and would be ceasing to return home for weekends. All this made Tom sad. He wondered, was it his boil? Or was it just him? Would I be capable of getting myself a girlfriend if I hadn't got the boil, maybe? he would often wonder.

Sometimes when that thought occurred to him, he would just sit in the dark and sob like a big girl. All he could see were the shapes of the kitchen utensils on the table and the random items of furniture throughout the room – so shadowy and indistinct that they often made him wonder, would he be like that too, soon? A silhouette sitting on a chair, no longer of this world? And never in all his time on this earth having known the pleasure of a woman? He felt that he was a disgrace and that it was shameful for him to call himself a man, to even think of doing so. Sometimes when he considered this, Tom

Gully would cry. Then his dog Napper would come up to him and whimper and he would try to elucidate his troubles for the animal but, try as he might, he could never seem to find the proper words. Which upset him even more. Because he loved Napper. 'O, Napper,' he wept one day as he hugged the sad-eyed collie's tatty fur, 'I love you so much you'll never know because I am so useless that the words are all tangled up inside me like briars and I can't get at them.'

Once or twice, Tom felt like putting an end to the whole thing. 'It's a waste of time, that's what it is,' he said to himself and paused for a moment to consider the tin of Paraquat weedkiller he knew to be located in the outhouse. But, fortu-nately, he proceeded no further with this idea, and conse-quently the following afternoon was to be found sitting, once more, on the high stool in Shamey's, sipping his stout and wondering, in a chin-scratching moment of philosophy, what for the love of God had gotten into Shamey, the way he had destroyed his good pub. An observation which he didn't really in his heart and soul believe – had simply said it, in fact, because all the other farmers did. Because, after all, it had to be admitted that the disco (exotically named RA! RA'S!) brought plenty of women from outside and, with whom – if you played your cards right – well, who knew? The old bar was still the same, of course, with all the faded football photos and boxing stars lined up on the walls as they had been for years – but the back lounge? O, for God's sake, stop! thought Tom to himself, smiling broadly. No wonder he had to be drunk to go into it! They even had films on the walls now (black singers in sunglasses and shiny suits, if you don't mind!) and lights that made you think you had dust all over your jacket! It was just when Tom was thinking this that out of the corner of his eye he saw something that made him remark –

silently of course – to himself: 'Jeepers! I think there must be something in this stout. Perhaps I'd better lay off it for a while!'

You have to remember, you see, that as yet it was only one thirty in the afternoon! And, although RA! RA'S! was due to open its doors that night, even the wildest women who came into Barntrosna, from Mullingar and various other places, to drink themselves senseless, didn't usually appear until at least seven thirty! Yet now, here was one of the most stunning, heavily made-up and perfume-drenched women Tom Gully had ever seen in his whole life! Sitting directly across from him and tapping on the glass with long crimson fingernails!

*

When he was younger, Tom's mother used to say to him: 'When you're big, love, and you find yourself in what you consider a difficult situation – particularly with girls – what I want you to do is say three Hail Marys for holy purity.' Somewhere deep within him, Tom felt sure that that was probably good advice. But somewhere also, quite close to the surface, it seemed, there was a voice that insistently repeated: 'Pay no heed to that old nonsense! Listen to me! Listen to me, Tom Gully! Don't be a fool! It's time to live, my boy! Time to live – and no better time to start!'

If anyone had been curious as to why, for no apparent reason, a great big grin appeared all of a sudden on the face of the heavy-set farmer at that precise moment, they would have found the answer in that very thought. And also in the image that, quite unexpectedly, followed on the heels of it. That of Tom Gully in a pair of dark glasses exactly like those favoured by the dancers in the films they projected on the walls at RA! RA'S! Resulting in his considering leaning over to the young woman to whisper in her ear: 'I was wondering, ma'am? Would you like a bottle of something?' Which Tom, because he knew himself and his own habits so well, was aware that there wasn't a hope in a million of him *actually* saying unless he applied himself with steely diligence to the task of consuming as many bottles of stout accompanied by as many brandy chasers as might be humanly possible. A task towards which he was now spurred on by the undulating curves of perfume that came sailing past directly beneath his nostrils, not to mention the whisper-crash of silk as two legs were once again crossed and a husky voice to the barman cooed: 'Excuse me, darling! May I have another Bacardi, please?'

When he heard this, it was all Tom Gully could do not to splutter the contents of his glass all down the front of his jacket. For in his mind he kept hearing that sentence repeat itself. Deep within him, there was a lighthouse and those were the words it beamed across the water. Over and over across the water. Tom suddenly felt dizzy. Nails! Crimson! And those pants! With spangles all over them, glittering away like glass in the sun. O, but that hair! Oo, that hair! (It was a pageboy cut but Tom didn't know that. And didn't care, either!) All he wanted to do with her hair was kiss it. Kiss it and run his fingers through it and say: 'O ma'am, I love your hair! I love it to bits, I'm telling you!'

Then – a shiver went running through him. He had forgotten his boil! He almost cried out: 'What if she doesn't like my boil?' Instantly he found himself on the verge of weeping and ordered two more brandy chasers. Within seconds, he felt good again. Good? He felt absolutely fantastic! The question he was now asking himself was: 'What boil?'

131

Tom couldn't see any boil. If someone was talking about boils, it must be boils on someone else's poor unfortunate head they were talking about. Just who was the happiest, most contented man in the village of Barntrosna right at that very moment? The answer to that question is: Tom Gully. There could be absolutely no doubt about it. Certainly, he was a big, heavy-set man with a boil on his forehead and a somewhat casual attitude, perhaps, to personal hygiene, but as far as inner peace and feelings of self-worth were concerned, Tom Gully was now a paradigm. Which was why he had no difficulty whatsoever in sliding from one seat to the next to find himself – in Ray-Ban sunglasses no less! (as it now, thanks to the rapidity of his consumption, appeared to him!) – sitting directly opposite a beautiful young lady chipped out of china! Who didn't seem to mind in the least, it has to be said. Affording him, in fact, just the tiniest of approving smiles! Which Tom Gully just could not believe, quite frankly! For he had not – not in a million years – expected it all to be so easy! For a split second he wondered – could it be a trick? And then almost wept when it became clear that it was not. 'Why yes – I think I would rather like another Bacardi,' she softly replied. Tom Gully felt as if he had just been elected President of Ireland. He could not stop himself hoping that the door would open and someone he knew – anyone – would arrive in and see him sitting there. This did not happen but it didn't matter – Tom Gully was still happy. Happy? It is a word which doesn't even come close to describing the state of inner excitement which Tom Gully was experiencing at that moment! He could not for the life of him believe the effect her voice was having on him. The sound of it was a magic melody in his ears. And she seemed so interested in everything! In what was going on around the village, when they had done up Shamey's place,

132

expectations for the coming tourist season, and so on. All of a sudden, Tom found himself transformed into the village spokesman. Which he was more than happy to be. Interesting facts regarding the local area poured from his lips in a torrent. When he went to the toilet, he was terrified on his return that she would be gone. His head was reeling as he searched for her through the haze. 'She's gone! Vanished!' he cried, and then he saw her, tapping ash into the tray. 'Mandy!' he cried in a weak falsetto, for that, she had informed him, was her name.

It was quite amusing when they were leaving the bar and Tom fell across one of the high stools. 'O, now, Tom!' Shamey gently chided him. 'You'll have to mind yourself now, you and them auld brandy chasers!' Tom pawed the air and smiled bashfully as his new companion helped him up. 'Thank you, Mandy!' he said and felt himself melting as she mischievously whispered: 'You great big thing you, Tom Gully!'

Tom was a little bit ashamed to be bringing her back to his crumbly old house but she assured him it didn't matter. In fact he had spent so long apologizing in advance that he was somewhat amazed she hadn't turned around and left him already. Which was why he kept repeating: 'I love you, Mandy,' as he went and stumbled across the step. Having to be assisted by her once again! 'O, you silly!' she said and chuckled. 'I love the way you say that,' he said. And he did! He could have listened to her saying it all night long! 'O, you silly, O you silly,' he said, and they both laughed as they went inside.

Napper was pleased to see them home, jumping up on his master's chest and licking him all over his face. Not knowing, of course, what to make of this new visitor. But not complaining either, because he could see it was perfectly plain she was being kind to his master. Kind? It was as if she had known him for years, for Heaven's sake! Even longer than Napper himself!

What Tom could not for the life of him understand was – why was she so interested in him? Why on earth would a woman so beautiful want to know a thing about Tom Gully? Those were the thoughts running through his mind as Tom lay spreadeagled in the chair, like a gigantic soft toy. How many times had he thus reclined, he asked himself, in that damp and mouldy kitchen, listening to the radio just as they were doing now, and dreaming this very scene, except never in a million years expecting it to be so close and tender? He felt perhaps he was losing his reason. Yes! That was it! He was going exquisitely, beautifully, mad in the head!

'So tell me then, Tom,' her voice whispered, 'do you like me? Do you like your little Mandy?'

Tom wanted to press his fingers to his eyes. He wanted to hide as he tried to find the courage to say to her: 'Miss – Miss! Please ask me that again,' because the white nylon blouse with the ruffles on the cuffs she was dangling on the end of her shiny crimson fingernail was distracting him.

Look out, Tom! White flesh! White flesh! flashed a sign inside his mind.

But flesh there wasn't – not as yet. Nothing, only an elegantly sculpted hand that languidly traced its way across the mesh of a brassière's blackest lace.

'O, I feel so hot!' she sighed.

Tom tried frantically to think of news. *Any* news as she began to sway to the rhythm of the music. The music that was made by Margo and the Country Flavour. Except that some-how now it has been transmuted into a primeval, untamed drumbeat in Tom Gully's mind! As she effortlessly slides onto his lap!

O, naughty boy! O, wicked Tom Toms! Who sobs in his night-time lady's arms as out across the fields his cows and sheep go moo and baa. Crimson nails stroking his cheek as Tom Gully shivers with a fear that is so sweet he wants to die of it. Die of it right now as he puts his arms around her neck to kiss her alabaster skin.

'I love you, Mandy!' he says. 'You didn't even remark on my boil.'

'Go away,' she coos, 'naughty boil!'

Tom is quivering like a reed in the breeze. 'Marry me, Mandy!' he says. 'Marry me and I'll give you all my money!'

Already, Tom Toms' peepers are aglow! For she really is considering!

'All the money in the house and all the land I own!' he cries, curling one plump finger around a thumb.

'O, Tom Toms! I couldn't! I really couldn't!' flutters Mandy.

'Here!' cries Tom as a shoal of five-pound notes from a drawer to the ground goes floating.

'Oo! You are serious after all!' coos Mandy.

As ruffly blouse to ceiling it goes sailing and sparkly pants at once come swooshing down!

*

Now Tom Gully had never been in a situation before where his head it kept banging off the chair and his voice became so high-pitched that you would have easily been confused as to the nature of his gender. Neither had he ever felt, as he did some hours later, as if some enormous vacuum cleaner had come along and sucked from within him all the enzymes and juices and male fluids he had in his life possessed. For the very first time, his cheeks had become so flushed that it was actually impossible to determine where exactly his boil began and his face ended. Why, he was in such a state that it was a miracle he was able to speak at all! Uttering the words: 'Oh my God! What a beautiful woman you are, Mandy! Mandy, God love you!' in the voice of a valiant athlete who has just, against all odds, completed the decathlon. Not that it made any difference, however, for his declarations, sadly, fell on deaf ears, if cold stone floors can be described as having ears. There is a sensation which will be familiar to readers of urban myths and similar tales of travellers in foreign parts who awake in discomfiting surroundings to experience a feeling of mortal dread in the lower regions of the abdomen. Who will discover, to their horror, some time later, that their innermost organs – their kidneys as a rule – have been removed whilst they slept, in the most treacherous of backstreet larcenies. A not dissimilar feeling now overcame Tom Gully, as he repeatedly called out Mandy's name – but in vain, to be answered only by the thin Barntrosna breeze rattling the bolt on the swinging back door of his kitchen. As his weather-beaten hand sank itself deep into the penumbral regions of his trouser pocket, the cold realization dawned on him that they were indeed missing – not his kidneys, but the innumerable five-pound notes which had been, he thought, safely and securely deposited there. He felt like weeping.

'Come back! Come back, you! That money belongs to me!' he cried helplessly as he waved his fist at the night, his only response that provided by the reluctantly turned head of a sleepy-eyed Charolais bull.

*

Tom Gully was now beside himself. There is no other way of describing it. For three solid hours, he wept copious amounts of tears into the firegrate. 'You idiot, Tom Gully!' he reproached himself remorselessly. 'You stupid silly idiot! For that's all you are! You should have known she was only taking you for a ride! Now look at you! A disgrace! A disgrace to the name Gully, nothing more! Are you surprised you're devastated?'

Which he was – devastated, that is – but not half as much as he was when, only some days later, he stretched before the mirror after a hard day's work, and to his amazement, divined once more upon the flush expanse of his forehead, a shining, almost gloatingly triumphant – boil! A pink-red sphere of flesh that seemed to lean towards him like some eerie red eye and wink: 'Hello there, Tom!'

That was but the beginning. In the days that followed, such lesions were to become commonplace and soon it was as if Tom Gully was similar to some horrible mutation that had – ludicrous as it seems, in a place not noted for covert government research or comparable activity – somehow managed to come into contact with radioactive materials. And, had it not been for the efforts of his physician, Dr Joe McCaffrey, would almost certainly have taken his own life.

'No,' Dr Joe counselled, folding his stethoscope, 'the cause of your ailment is not mysterious radiation or anything like it – as you well know, Tom Gully!'

Dr Joe fixed his patient with a firm but benevolent gaze.

'She stole your money, didn't she?'

It was as if all the unbearable, pent-up fury that had been bottled up inside Tom Gully for weeks came roaring out in a huge tidal wave.

'Yes, doctor!' he cried as he sank his meaty fist into the

heart of his palm. 'Every penny! Every last penny I ever earned, she took it off me! It's true! Every word you've spoken is true!'

This was to be the beginning of the healing process for Tom Gully and, years later, whenever he would reflect on his ordeal, that evening in Dr Joe's surgery always featured as the very first point on the journey it had fallen to him to make – the 'long march towards recovery', as it were.

And whenever he would speak of it, to his neighbours, or while having a stout with Shamey in the bar, he would always smile wistfully – but not without a tinge of regret, for what might have been, perhaps – abstractedly fingering his last remaining boil beneath his shirt as he mused: 'Yes! She made a cod of me, and it's been a long road – but it's all over now! And it'll be a long time before she does it again, let me tell you!' before yet again taking his zinc buckets – a regular ritual now! – and heading off down the open road, swinging them gaily as he approached the dairy, meticulously positioning them as he stroked the flanks of the gentle heifer, who went 'moo' in eager anticipation, a contentment the like of which he'd never known settling at last upon Tom Gully as he adjusted his cap and, licking his lips, once more felt a broad proprietorial smile beginning to unwind across his bright, weather-beaten cheeks.

The Valley of
the Flying Jennets

I expect, now that Ireland has become such a changed place over the past few years, with European flags and coffee shops and contemporary artworks in the vanguard of this admittedly extraordinary cultural metamorphosis (not to mention the omnipresent chirp of portable phones and the industrious purr of facsimile machines), that there are many people – in particular those of the younger generation – who would find it very difficult to accept – in these new, empirical times – the story of the Valley of the Flying Jennets and who would most likely form the opinion that you fabricated the entire scenario, to further your own sadly egotistical ends. Were that to be the reaction I would not be in the least surprised, for even now, when I cast my mind back on those days, I have to occasionally reprimand myself lest I fall victim to the tendency of embellishing what was an otherwise unremarkable period of my life. For, in all honesty, it is not every day you hear of mythic creatures the like of which are to be encountered within the pages of this story, and indeed figure most prominently within it. As a matter of fact, it is well I recall the first occasion on which I broke my silence and related the tale to a few of my closest friends in the Georgian Room of the Barntrosna Arms Hotel one winter night in 1963. The expressions upon their collective countenances were far from what you might describe as 'transfixed'. I recall one of the less animated responses on that occasion being that of Barney Rafters, a farmer who has been in the livestock trade for generations, who was heard to cry: 'Aye! And my prize Aberdeen Angus has just given birth to a fucking monkey, Dr John Joe Parkes!'

But laugh as he might – and indeed his colleagues! – the more he attended to my tale, the more intrigued he found himself becoming – with the result that by the time we broke up in the deserted bar on that freezing November night there were very few of my companions who made their way home in their heavy topcoats and scarves believing that what I had spoken was anything other than the truth.

*

It all began some months after I had completed my final examinations – after some tedious three years of 'repeats' – in Trinity College, Dublin. I was residing with my parents in the family home, biding my time until an opportunity presented itself for me to begin a full-time practice and devote myself and whatever talents I might possess to the care of the community which I hoped would value them, and provide me with sufficient remuneration to keep body and soul together in the process. It was an innocent time in our little country, with nothing much happening from one day to the next bar the sound of asses and carts as they clip-clopped merrily past our window where I sat poring over my lexicons and medical charts, whilst my mother busied herself with her hot, steaming soda cakes, my father sonorously declaiming Yeats from his recumbent position in the chimney corner. Work there was certainly for me to do in my home place, but rarely did it extend beyond the world of superficial skin grazes or the preparation of poultices, for the more specific and complicated needs of the citizens of Barntrosna were already taken care of by Dr Heber O'Grady, not someone whom I myself would employ to attend to my needs, preferring indeed, if veracity is to be paramount here, to be attended to by a mentally deficient orang-utan. An appraisal which is not – I assure you, for I am above the tedious spite and petty back-biting which is a feature of village life, the medical profession being no more immune than any other – in any way connected with his repeated, would-be humorous asides, the moment I had my back turned, to the effect of: 'Yes, chaps! There he goes! Barntrosna's answer to Dr Christiaan Barnard, I don't think – ha ha ha! Good man, John Joe, you boy you! Did you get your exams yet?'

A lesser practitioner than I might have taken issue with him but I am not such a man. It has been suggested on occasion that the gentle disposition with which I am blessed is attributable to my predilection for opiates, which I feel is inaccurate, much as I may be partial to them ever since my days in Trinity, for the fact is that from my earliest years I have been, I feel, uncommonly slow to anger. I realize that there are those who, given such a degree of unwarranted provocation, would undoubtedly have reacted by hurling him to the pavement and raining bitter blows upon his superior tweeds. But such a course of action would not be that preferred by JJ Parkes, MD. If my character is anything, it is rational, even-tempered, sensible. Which makes what happened next all the stranger.

*

I was reclining in my study perusing some of the pages of Dr Freud and partaking of my little afternoon indulgence, which consisted of barely a fraction of the samples I had brought with me from my alma mater upon the termination of my studies there, when my father burst in with a sheet of paper in his hand, crying: 'JJ! You have been offered a position! Why, this is wonderful! At last someone in the house has got a job!'

My father (it was said of him that he considered himself above such mundane pursuits – had not worked in thirty years, devoting himself entirely to the declamation of verse in public places since his own graduation from that same aforementioned august institution) continued, perching his pince-nez on the bridge of his nose: 'But the oddest thing is – it's in a place I've never heard of!'

Such was my excitement I did not care a jot if I had been offered a position in Kathmandu or the Outer Hebrides. I leaped from my chair and, gripping the sheet of paper, read furiously in a trembling voice: 'On behalf of the community of Labashaca, I would like to take this opportunity to offer you the position of General Practitioner, to take effect immediately. Signed yours sincerely, Fr Tom Bannie.'

I could not believe my eyes. I landed my father a rough punch on his right shoulder and cried: 'I got it, Daddy! Do you realize what this means? Do you?' I could see that he was delighted for me and resolved to repair to my room and pack at once.

The saddest part of all was bidding farewell to my mother. I have always harboured a special affection for her, both of us consequently finding ourselves in floods of tears at the garden gate as the jarvey waited patiently for me. 'Please write to me, son! Write and tell me all about the people of Labashaca and your new-found friends!' she said. I assured her that I would. Then I said goodbye to my father and we were off. Johnnie Colcannon was the jarvey and he had been driving our family for generations so I felt I was in safe hands. That was my first mistake.

*

The last thing I remember before I fell asleep was a beautiful rose-red sky with the sun a shimmering orange ball hanging like a lamp between the sharp peaks of the distant Slieve Took mountains. But when I awoke both it and they had vanished and in their place were clouds of the oddest ink-blue hue that somehow seemed to possess just the slightest touch of menace, filling me throughout with a sense of the deepest foreboding. Which, I realized at once, was fanciful nonsense, and wholly due to the fact that our journey had already taken us some hours and that I had been overcome by a debilitating lassitude. I suppose it is fair to say that by my very rationality – upon which I pride myself, and always have – I effectively demolished my irrationality. And was about to observe as much to my good friend the jarvey, except that when he slowly turned to hear my words, I saw that it was not him but a smaller man who, whilst bearing a superficial resemblance to Johnnie Colcannon, my driver of some hours earlier, had within his skull set two bead-like eyes of such glassy emptiness that it could mean only one thing – the driver of my jaunting car and custodian of Ernest, our trusty trotting steed, had been spirited somehow away, and in his place installed – a *changeling*!

There are those who will claim that in the case of adults the removal of one person and their substitution with another who bears a vaguely similar yet somehow different aspect is, quite simply, an impossibility. But this is not the case. There have been many such instances. A well-to-do lady in Ballintack in 1892 returned to find her husband Martin's chair inhabited by a beguiling stranger with whom she had to spend the rest of her life, eventually being beaten to death by him in a row over cups and saucers. An ordinary housewife in the county of Cash lay in bed one night and awoke to see an empty-eyed stranger – who bore the swarthy features of her husband but did not speak with his voice – climbing in beside her and making illicit suggestions of the most repellent kind. The evidence is ample, to say the very least. And now – here I was! – sharing a car with a jarvey who was not my own. A clammy hand of fear took hold of me and I swore I should never reach Labashaca alive.

*

Which, fortunately, I did, but whether, considering the fate that lay in store for me, 'fortunately' is the appropriate word or not is a moot point, for hardly had I arrived at the door of the hotel than I was approached by an oily-looking individual in a hacking jacket who let it be known that his name was Albert Huntingdon. I smiled as best I could, having no interest whatsoever in either him or his name, and was about to tip my cap and push past him into the hotel when I found myself pinned up against a wall and as malevolent an eye as ever I encountered bit into me as sharp and as deep as any sword. 'Don't think I don't know who you are, Mr JJ Parkes, so-called practitioner in the field of medicinal arts! And don't think I don't know you are a direct descendant of Fortescue Hastings-Parkes, would-be veterinary surgeon and part-time scientist, who has visited a scourge on the town of Labashaca that no amount of forgiveness can ever wash away! You would do well to remember that, Mr Dr JJ!'

*

As I breathlessly slumped to the tarmacadamed forecourt, I looked up to see my bulky assailant disappearing with a shuffle into the dark. I was bewildered, his harsh words still ringing in my ears. For I did indeed have a relative by the name of Fortescue Hastings-Parkes, a pioneer in the field of animal medicine, who had disappeared without trace in the late 1890s, and who was rarely spoken of now, as though his name were tainted by some horrendously unspeakable shame. As I hauled myself aloft and once more gripped my travelling bags, I was about to consider this ravelled web of perplexity when to my ears there drifted the coarse sound of mocking laughter and I looked up to see the writhing, corballed face of the changeling observing me from the shadows of an alleyway where he had stalled his jaunting car, his mouth a lopsided aperture from which this indulgent chuckling emerged, his pocket jangling with the sound of the coins he had wilily extricated from me earlier. When I looked again, he was gone. As indeed was the hotel, which only minutes before had been standing directly in front of me and was now entirely relocated, brick by brick, on the opposite side of the square. I stumbled across the tarmac, tired and exhausted, unable to probe these mysteries further and, with all the strength I could muster, provided the receptionist with my name and details and made my way upstairs to bed.

*

Throughout that night I found myself assailed by strange dreams. I saw myself standing by a withered tree, holdall in hand, as if anxiously waiting for someone. Which, it transpired, I was indeed, as moments later an autobus came to a halt directly in front of the withered tree. I was astonished to find myself confronted by what appeared to be a middle-aged man in plus-fours and Edwardian jacket, but which was impossible for me to say for certain as he had no face. Surely, I feel assured I hear you murmur, he must have had some face! But no. In all sincerity, reader, I tell you – in this case, of face, or features even approximating thereto, not the slightest trace was evident. And yet, somehow, I heard him speak! I heard the words, as he extended his beautifully manicured hand to me, clear and mellifluous as a stream flowing on a bright summer's day: 'Good day! My name is Fortescue Hastings-Parkes. Come with me!'

Within minutes, I found myself transported to the interior of the most magnificent edifice. Through the opened French windows the plangent melodies of Schubert drifted out across the splendid gardens, above which towered the leafy shape of a large horse, to which a bent and aged figure was putting the finishing touches. 'O'Hagan, our topiarist,' explained Fortescue. As he spoke, a large red setter came bounding along the hall and pinned me to the wall, licking me furiously about the face and ears. 'Fergus,' cried Fortescue, 'stop that!'

I was relieved when the animal withdrew its paws and sat like a lamb in the centre of the floor. 'Yes,' continued Fortescue as we made our way towards the library, 'I have many things to tell you, Dr JJ! Many things!'

As I turned to face him, I was astonished to find that his face had almost entirely returned, and even more perplexed as I realized, now that it was fully formed, it was what you would describe as an almost perfect replica of my own! As we stood there beneath the packed bookshelves, sipping a tincture of the finest port it has ever been my privilege to taste, I might have been engaged in conversation with my twin. 'Yes, dear JJ,' he continued, 'I have many things to explain. Tell me – has it ever occurred to you why you possess such a sense of – how shall I put it? – "class" – of what perhaps we might call "breeding"? And yet all your life you have spent in a tiny ramshackle cottage in which there is barely room to swing a cat? Has it never occurred to you that you, like some of these poor creatures who claim they are women trapped in the bodies of men, are a blue-blooded landowning fellow, of the finest, purest extraction, marooned in what can only be called a habit of the coarsest, most mundane flesh? Have you never asked yourself: "Why am I called John Joe? Why is my name not Erskine? Or Johnston? Or Ivan Percival? Vernon, perhaps?" Mm?'

He observed me fixedly and I am sure he heard my heart miss a beat. How many times as I lay in my bed had I asked myself these questions? How many times as the rough words of the village corner boys came once more to my ears in such phrases as 'Good man, John Joe!' and 'Take it handy, Squire John Joe!' had I asked myself those very same questions? Why, from the very day I was born, had I not felt as they did, and instead perceived myself as 'chosen'? Why did my grandfather, until the end of his days, stare at me with such sadness, a broken and decrepit white-haired man old before his time, crippled upon a crooked stick because of some dark secret in which the world could not be permitted to share? It was all I could do not to hide my face beneath my coat. For if anyone had ever released a dart that found its mark in the centre of someone's heart, in that single moment, Fortescue Hastings-Parkes had.

*

The following morning, at table, when I perceived that it was the intention of my fellow diners to be less than civil, I

149

decided at once that I would not permit myself to be in the slightest way intimidated by them and resolved to continue as genial a conversation as was possible in the circumstances, passing comments on the quality of the comestibles, toast and the various other items of foodstuffs which it had fallen to us to dispose of that morning. But it was all to no avail and, in the end, I found that I could contain myself no longer, rising to my feet and slamming my knife and fork down on my plate, crying: 'Damn you all! What is the matter with you! And just what the hell is going on in this village!' If I felt that this outburst might produce some reaction, I was but a fool! For all the reaction I provoked I might as well have been sitting alongside people made entirely of sponge or straw. With whatever equanimity I could muster, I finished what remained of my breakfast, dabbed the stain of egg yolk that had lodged itself upon my tie and made my way out into the morning.

I had all but gone ten yards when I felt a hand touch my shoulder. Instinctively I turned. 'Fortescue!' I cried. But the small round man shook his head. 'No,' he said, 'my name is Considine. Tom Considine. I am informed I am to be your partner here in the village.' When I heard those words, a huge sense of relief came over me. Such was my unease since my arrival in Labashaca that had I turned and discerned before my eyes an Indian warrior or Nazi war criminal I should not have been in the least surprised. Now, for the very first time since my arrival, I found myself in the company of someone I felt I could trust implicitly. Which was foolhardy in the extreme, for, as it transpired, Tom Considine was not only a hopeless incompetent, but also a mean, spiteful, and wholly disreputable individual who would stop at nothing in order to line his pockets so that he might feed his vile habit. Which, I was very soon to learn, involved the consumption of ludicrously inordinate quantities of alcohol. I am by no means prudish by nature, and have no objections whatsoever to the inhalation of a regular opium cigarette or quiet disposal of that substance in tablet form, but such was my partner's reliance on these vast volumes of liquid intoxicants that it became only a matter of time before I grew to despise him. Hardly had we been installed in the beautiful office which, as he explained, we were to share, overlooking the main street and the blue cloud-necklaced mountains that encircled Labashaca, than his manner toward me began to change – ever so slightly at first, but, without a doubt, with enough significance not to go unnoticed. Initially he would debate enthusiastically with me regarding various ailments particular to the town, advising me on the most appropriate manner in which to deal with certain patients, and going into great detail about any number of exotic illnesses, of which I knew little or nothing, I admit. And I could only marvel at the undiluted breadth of his knowledge as he paced the office floor in his starched white coat. A starched white coat that slowly but surely became a crumpled grey pile dumped in a corner beneath a faded chart depicting the labyrinthine complexity of the human anatomy as my so-called partner and 'superior' reached deep into his pocket to produce a twenty-pack of Major cigarettes (acknowledged in the medical profession as the strongest available on the market) and, proceeding to light one for himself, audaciously requested 'the loan of twenty pounds'. I presumed that its return would be forthcoming later, and thought no more of it. Little did I know that this was but the beginning. Before the week was out, I had parted with the sum of not less than one hundred and twenty-seven pounds, and was slowly beginning to realize that in all likelihood I would never lay eyes upon those monies again. Especally when, upon my return to the hotel late one night, I heard a familiar voice call from across the street: 'Oi! John Joe! Are you all right for a few quid?' and looked over to see, not, at first, my medical partner, but a rotund, red-faced man whose face was a mass of sundered capillaries – clearly a knight of the road: behind whom lurked my so-called colleague, doing his level best to conceal himself, the unmistakable sound of chuckling emanating from behind his nicotine-stained fingers.

It was to be some weeks before I was to discover the sickening truth that 'Dr' Tom Considine was not, in fact, a doctor at all, and that the coat in which he had been parading so confidently had been secretly removed from the local hospital some days before my arrival. When I confronted him with this, he merely laughed, slamming the door behind him and calling back – or should I say snarling back – that I was 'Daft! Like all the Parkeses!' and that I would 'get what was coming to me around Labashaca' for what it was I had supposedly done!

As I sat there in the deafening stillness of the late afternoon, staring at the pile of weathered brown folders and coloured pamphlets which arrived daily (the only colour evident in my rapidly greying life at that time), try as I might, I could not still his words, each one tapping away at the base of my cranium as if a tiny metal hammer with a mind and a mechanism all of its own. What did he mean by that? Why did I feel so strange since my arrival in Labashaca? Why had I not been visited by one single patient since setting up my practice? Did in fact a village named Labashaca even exist? I asked myself. By the time I left the building that evening, I was on the point of collapse.

*

152

On many occasions I have wondered what might have become of me if I had not been fortunate enough that very evening to encounter a person who, to this day, remains a loyal and trusted friend, and whose calm, reasoned and gentle ways proved to be the key which finally unlocked the 'Mystery of Labashaca'. I found myself in a state of extreme anxiety, particularly after my encounter with my jarvey, who appeared out of the dark as I stumbled hotelward, addressing me with the sinister words: 'Do you think you'll be needing me to drive you home, sir?' and disappearing once more into the dark as I cried out with all my might: 'What is wrong with you? What are you trying to do? Are you trying to drive me mad? What have I done on you, damn you! What have I done!'

*

Such was my despair as I sat at the counter of the hotel bar that night that when a clammy hand was laid upon my shoulder I instinctively whirled and, with my fists squared, cried, 'Damn you to hell! All of you!' only to see before me the tweed-coated figure of a white-moustached man in his sixties, a walking cane elegantly suspended from his pocket, and upon his head a pork-pie hat of expensive Donegal herringbone, its pointed beak momentarily obscuring his bushy eyebrows. I observed him as best I could through eyes that were the equivalent of fogged-up windscreens in the wildest of blizzards. He extended his hand, removing his calf-leather glove before he did so. 'Oxford Cathcart, at your service,' he said. It is sad to report that I greeted his extended hand by issuing forth a number of the foulest expletives, pushing him away as if he were some unacceptable person ravaged by contagious disease. 'Go away!' I snapped. 'I want nothing to do with you or anyone else from this godforsaken dump!'

153

At this, heads turned and I found myself facing any number of sets of malevolent eyes. But I was beyond regret. 'Go on, then! Look!' I cried, with all the acidic unpleasantness I could muster. 'That's all you're good for around here, isn't it, you stupid fools! Look at you, all of you! More chance of finding brains in a jennet!'

As I uttered those words, a hysterical scream rent the air and the last thing I remember is a vase of flowers becoming airborne and sailing towards me through the air, smashing into a million pieces against the wall behind me. As a vast creature (he can only be called a 'labouring type') flung himself in my direction, I heard the familiar voice of Oxford Cathcart cry: 'Run, man! For the love of God, run!' as he grabbed my arm and pulled me onward, both of us fleeing into the night.

*

I must have passed out at that point for the next thing I remember is waking up in the most sumptuous of surroundings, with Oxford by my bedside dabbing my forehead with a cool cloth. I made to get up but he cautioned me, with all the tenderness and consideration that are the characteristics of the man. 'What happened?' I asked him, and his features clouded over like a small rock pool whose implacable tranquillity is disturbed by a small stone or pebble cast into its depths. He sighed, and sinking his hands deep in the pockets of his dragon-festooned dressing gown, faced the wall opposite and, without turning, said: 'You made a big mistake in that hotel bar last night, John Joe.'

There ensued a long spell of silence.

'But how, Oxford? Why?' I replied.

'Because,' he continued, 'of all the words you can utter in

the town of Labashaca, there is none more feared or despised than that of "jennet".'

I considered for a moment and then said: 'Oh, come now, Cathcart. Surely you must be joking. What harm can there possibly be in including the name of a harmless dumb animal who is but a cross between a mare donkey and a pony in an otherwise unspectacular sentence?'

'I am not joking, John Joe!' he replied, to my astonishment with one deft movement removing in its entirety all his facial hair, including his wig, crying: 'Does the name Fortescue Hastings-Parkes mean anything to you?' as I felt the blood running from my face and gazed upon the man who now stood trembling before me – a man known only as Fortescue Hastings-Parkes!

I gasped, trying to find the words to express my disbelief!

'Yes, it is me, John Joe!' he continued. 'I wanted it to happen some other way – but after last night, I have no option!'

'But . . . but, I don't understand! What harm could there possibly be in saying . . . jennet?'

'You didn't just say jennet, John Joe! What you actually said was – you'd find more *brains* in a *jennet*!'

'Yes, Oxford . . . but . . .!'

'Get your things. We're going for a ride!' he declaimed authoritatively.

*

Within minutes, we were bounding through open countryside on ebony-black steeds, Fortescue Hastings-Parkes instinctively slicing through foliage and undergrowth like the noble, determined horseman that he was. It was approaching nightfall when we reached our destination, a secluded valley to the north of Labashaca, a place so ineffably quiet it almost brought your heart to a standstill. 'Fortescue,' I began, but was silenced by an expressionless hand. 'Ssh,' he whispered and then I heard it, for the first time that night. A time that was to be followed by many others that night before dawn would break. 'Do you hear it?' he said. I nodded and cocked my ear to listen again. '*Nnngyeeagh! Cheep! Nnngyeeagh! Cheep!*' as alien a sound as ever it has been my experience to hear, emanating from the vast blue table mountain framed against the light-flecked black velvet of the night sky. 'Let us make a fire,' said Fortescue, 'for we have to talk, you and I!'

I gave myself to the task of gathering some kindling and producing flame with the aid of two small twigs and, within the hour, Fortescue was ready to begin his tale. A tale which, initially, I confess, prompted me on a number of occasions towards the words: 'Surely you must be kidding, Fortescue!', 'Really, Fortescue!', and 'Oh, yes! I'm sure!'

Little did I realize that what I was soon to witness would haunt me for the rest of my mortal days.

As he filled the pipe which he produced from the inside pocket of his tweed coat, my scholarly companion continued: 'This may be very difficult to believe, and if at times you find my story too much for you to bear, I implore you, please – do not hesitate to stop me. But, John Joe, rest assured that every word I speak here tonight is true. Do you understand me?'

I nodded as best I could, such was my emotional and physical fatigue after all I had been through. A sizeable lump of tobacco was once again packed into the bowl of his fluted briar as he began anew in a barely audible voice, which seemed with every syllable to grow ever more tremulous and agitated. Nevertheless, the pattern of his most extraordinary narrative began to take shape, in that lonely copse on all sides bounded by mountains, the flames of our little fire moving this way and that as though instinctively providing a lyrical counterpoint to the twists and turns of the tale.

'You may have seen pictures of my grandfather, also Fortescue Hastings-Parkes, who was a noted Victorian biologist, biochemist and physician. In his time, he was responsible for many of the major developments in science and medicine. To this day, many of his learned tomes and papers are to be found in museums and libraries and universities all over the world. But, John Joe—'

I paled as Fortescue leaned closer to me and I felt his hot breath on my cheek.

'Very few,' he went on, 'very few of his admirers know or realize that for every one of his experiments and investigations, which seemed, admirably, to advance the cause of science, there was invariably one that went most horribly wrong!'

I gasped, and was instinctively withdrawing from the disquieting information that was being offered to me when, quite unexpectedly, this erudite weaver of words proceeded to produce from his pocket what initially I took to be a scroll but which, it transpired, was an oil painting, bearing some signs of wear and tear but in an otherwise perfectly acceptable state, and which, to my complete and utter astonishment, depicted, in my companion's words: 'A Man With No Face!'

I was rendered completely and utterly speechless as I gazed upon the image and recognized instantly the figure from my dream of that first night in the hotel – the figure of what could only be my relative Fortescue Hastings-Parkes – *without his face*! I longed for the tale to reach its conclusion. How I prayed that it would! But we Parkeses are not known for limp and lacklustre narratives, thus onward he proceeded, my by now almost fevered storytelling relative. 'Yes,' he cried, 'such as this one! An experiment which, in theory, was to revolutionize medicine, a form of cosmetic surgery, if you like, known only to him, and which was to result in the complete realignment and astonishing improvement of his features – but succeeded only in the complete and utter removal of his face!'

I gasped as he uttered the words.

'But that, my dear relative,' he went on, 'is as nothing to the hideous transgression for which you and I, generations later, are still paying the penalty!'

'Generations? Penalty?' I stammered, as I felt his hand on my arm.

'Come with me,' he said softly.

So lightheaded and confused did I find myself, it was all I could do to follow him across that nocturnal plain and up the side of the mountain until we attained a plateau, whereupon we rested a moment and gathered our strength before he said: 'What you are about to see has not been witnessed by any of our family since those dark Labashaca days when the noble efforts of Fortescue Hastings-Parkes on behalf of his community resulted in a disaster so unimaginably vast, so unutterably repellent that mere words, to this day, cannot begin to describe it.'

'Words? Describe?' I cried, hoarsely.

'Yes!' he snapped. 'Yes, JJ! Yes! Come!'

I stumbled after him as he strode decisively towards the edge of the plateau. Within seconds, I found myself looking down into the valley, my eyes meeting a scene which to this day fills me with such horror and revulsion that I can hardly bear to describe it. For there, shadowed against the blunt vastness of the table mountain (it seemed like some enormous cardboard cutout), were creatures so pathetic in their aspect that no diabolic hand or claw could possibly, I reflected, have fashioned them. Not only that but, along with their vile physicality, they seemed to possess no natural intelligence whatsoever, charging wildly in all directions, flying upside down and generally ululating sounds which were neither identifiably equine nor aviatory. One of the sad creations even flew close to my face, crying, '*Nngyeaagh! Cheep!*' in a manner that was, whilst infuriatingly irritating, in its own peculiar way, shot through with the oddest of melancholies. After some minutes of their mindless, patternless and wholly illogical behaviour – one of them relentlessly pounded a whin bush with its back legs until nothing remained but a tattered, broken mess and then flew off into the clouds – backways, of course – as though with a sense of incontestable triumph – I could take no more, stumbling awkwardly across the plateau with my hand covering my eyes. 'Yes,' my companion said, resting his hand gently on my shoulder, 'now you know the truth. That is why the people of Labashaca hate us and why for successive generations nothing but bad fortune has befallen us. For those . . . creatures, if you can call them such, John Joe, my friend, were once as you and me. The ancestors of some law-abiding, good-natured Labashaca folk who perhaps were too trusting in their dealings with my grandfather. Naive, credulous innocents whose good nature led them to – that! Whose hunger for immortality, perhaps, induced them to risk everything. Everything, John Joe!'

I lowered my head in shame as he proceeded. 'You see, John Joe, he assured them he could transform them into angels. That they would live for all eternity. In fairness, part of his promise he did in fact fulfill – the wings you have just seen are proof of that! But he had not accounted for a local animal – a jennet, of course! – which had rambled up the north face of the mountain at the very moment whilst the experiment was being conducted! In any case, to make a long story short – for I can see you are both physically and mentally exhausted, John Joe, and I do not blame you! – as I am sure you are aware, all radiated energy has a dual nature. Not only does it emanate as waves, but also in short bursts it is measured in quanta. However, to measure both speed and position simultaneously involves a large degree of possible error. This is known, after its discoverer, as Heisenberg's Uncertainty Principle, and has much bearing upon the tragic error of our tale: the breakage of chromosomes, in effect, so that their characteristics are not passed on in reproduction – mutations, in a word – hastened by the appearance, at a critical moment in the experiment, of the hapless creature which lumbered into view, my grandfather having already activated the ultraviolet radiation ionizer which was to effect the transformation of human flesh into celestial epidermis – and having actually seen the foolish beast, but a fraction of a second too late! A cry of despair issued from his lips and, instantaneously, the valley was filled with a blinding light and the screech of the most unintelligent animal ever visited upon this earth. With a poignant falling of feathers from the sky, all within seconds was over, and what you have witnessed in the valley below is the heartbreaking, devastating result. Now do you understand, my dear, dear relative, how it is that the house of Hastings-Parkes has been afflicted for all these years?'

I felt tears well up in my eyes as a neighing, chirruping jennet ascended the lip of the plateau and sailed close by my shoulder. Within minutes, we were both weeping copiously, whilst below in the valley, the raucous cacophony – an absurd tournament of jousting whistles and snorts (as though some form of rudimentary phonetic mockery) – became more than we could endure and at once we began our journey back to the town of Labashaca.

*

I took my leave of the town very soon afterwards and to this day have not laid eyes upon my learned, misfortunate blood relative. Thus, I have no means of substantiating this tale for those readers who might be of a sceptical nature, surreptitiously adverting to 'lassitudinous days in Trinity', perhaps, or 'excessive consumption of white powders and opium tablets'.

Even were he to present himself for those purposes, I fear I could not find it within myself to prevail upon him to relate anew the horrors experienced by us that night upon the plateau. No, I have laid the facts before my readers for them to make of them what they will. I realize that in these days of 'information superhighways', exotic bottled beers and video disc players, tales involving lost valleys, vanished relatives and ludicrous equine-angel hybrids will most likely be dismissed as nonsense. If that is indeed the case, then so be it. In response, all I can say is that, to this day, not one of the Parkes family is fortunate to live in a decent house, or bear a dignified name (shame has decreed that we shall all be appelled 'Bunty', 'Mickey', 'Bridie', and – most loathsome of all – 'John Joe!'), for my own part, my residence, since I resigned my practice, being a derelict shack on the outskirts of Barntrosna, my sanity preserved only by the occasional indulgence in a little cigarette or perhaps a tablet or two. The image of Fortescue Hastings-Parkes still resides proudly upon my mantelpiece, praying – no doubt! – that I will not one day turn to find its visage completely blank and obliterated, just as I do that I will not one day innocently gaze outside my window and there locate a dead-eyed, obstinate creature, complete with haplessly flapping, entirely unlaundered wings, staring back at me as though some thoroughly redundant, sympathy-craving, bargain-bin Pegasus. For that, dear reader, would be, I assure you, more than I, John Joe Parkes MD (retd.), would be humanly capable – and here, please, I implore you, do not judge me too harshly – *Puff! Puff! Choke! Choke!* – of enduring.

The Forbidden Love of
Noreen Tiernan

Mrs Tiernan, Noreen's mother, was well known in Barntrosna as a woman who could 'turn her hand to anything' and was on more committees and boards than anyone could begin to remember. But it still came as a shock when she immersed herself in what later became known as 'The Noreen Tiernan Affair' with an obsessive fury. There were those who said that if her husband, Oweny James, had still been alive it would never have happened. But how can we possibly know? Who is to say that he too, on discovering the truth about his beloved daughter, would not also have abandoned everything and caught the next available flight to London? Love is no bed-fellow of reason.

And Noreen Tiernan was loved, and loved deeply – let there be no mistake about that. Ever since her days as a young girl strolling about the streets and byways and butterfly-populated lanes of Barntrosna, her gap-toothed smile had been the delight of all the hard-working farmers, who would cry as she passed: 'There you are now, Noreen! Lovely day, thank God! How's your father?'

'He's very well, thank you,' Noreen would shyly reply. Sometimes they would lean on their hayforks and marvel after her: 'God, but isn't she growing up to be the powerful young girl, all the same! Oweny James Tiernan should be a proud man this day!'

As indeed he was, and in the years before he passed away tragically after misjudging his footing while negotiating

McCracken's drain late one night on his way home from the Bridge Bar, it was not uncommon to hear him, as he fixed a single, determined eye on the invariably considerable length of ash that extended precariously from his Player's cigarette, remark: 'You won't get a better girl in this world than our wee Noreen, eh? What do you say, men?'

Whereupon his fellow parishioners, as with one voice, would cry: 'Now you're talking, Oweny James. You're talking now and no mistake!'

Beneath the sign for Capstan Plug in the half-light of those summer evenings the consensus would be absolute. Noreen was truly incomparable, as with each day that passed she assumed the features of nothing less now than a world-famous beauty queen. As one Thomas Hartigan, a neighbour of hers and something of a poet, observed one day, there were times when the light slanted across her face that you wouldn't think you were looking at eyes at all but two precious stones set in a head carved from finest ivory.

By the time she reached sixteen years of age, the beauty of Noreen Tiernan had become so striking that whenever she walked down the main street of Barntrosna all the men who lined the corner would stare after her in stunned silence. As Jackie Burdon said on one occasion, shaking his head: 'If young Tiernan doesn't turn out to be an international model, I'll eat all my winter silage.'

*

But Noreen Tiernan didn't have the slightest intention of becoming a model of any kind, international or otherwise. As anyone who had bothered to take the time to ask her would have learnt. This was because she had known from a very early age when her father – ironically, under the impression he was immersed in a thrilling Western story (his one passion – he made it his business to read at least a half-dozen per week) entitled *Forty Guns to Apache Pass* somehow managed to read aloud to her a significant section of the life of Florence Nightingale, filling her with the deepest admiration for the English nurse whose selflessness throughout the Crimean War was legendary. As her father continued reading in the firelight, rocking back and forth on his chair and punctuating the narrative with anachronistic and wholly illogical snippets of frontier vernacular along the lines of *'ornery'* and *'critters'*, Noreen could see herself standing, in her crisply starched uniform, over any number of broken, helpless men, briskly administering tonics and medicines as they reached out to her – futilely, for all in Noreen's eyes were equal – courting preferential treatment in frail, hoarse voices. As she sat there in the shadows, she thought of herself sometime in the future, clapping her hands smartly and chirping to the other nurses, 'Come along, staff! There's work to be done here!' rigid and unshakeable as a Doric column as her subordinates filed past her with eyes downcast, but with hearts full of affection – and, most of all, respect.

There were times too when she would envisage herself on the remote, baked plains of the Australian outback, landing the rickety craft that was the flying doctor plane and dashing through the dust with her medicine bag flapping as a plaintive cry echoed somewhere in the bush.

And often, too, it cannot be denied, in the arms of a close-shaven, handsome young doctor, who as they danced to the music of Frank Sinatra or Tony Bennett would touch the soft lobes of her ears with his lips and gently whisper: 'How I love you, Queen of the Ward! My sweet and wonderful, wonderful Noreen Tiernan.'

No, that was why, Noreen knew, she would never be a top model. Not for her the vulgar assault of flashing bulbs and prying lenses, the facile, ill-informed and essentially exploitative interrogations of supercilious chatshow hosts. For her, she knew only too well, the catwalks of Europe would be but as highways to nowhere.

To appear, however unostentatiously, within the pages of *Nursing Times* was her sole ambition.

Which was why when, at the age of seventeen years, she learned that she had been accepted as a trainee nurse into St Bartholomew's General Hospital, Chiswick, London, she was absolutely over the moon! She stood in the middle of the floor in the kitchen of the Tiernans' simple four-room cottage and cried: 'I got it! I got it, Mammy! I've been accepted into St Barty's!'

Her mother smiled and thought to herself how pleased Oweny James (ten years dead that very week – the anniversary Mass was due to take place, as usual, close by McCracken's drain where they had placed the wooden cross which read: *I. M. Oweny James – tragically drowned on this spot Sept. 7 1970*) would have been if he had been there to see it. To witness all his children, Ta and Willie and Wee Patty, clustered about the skirts of his eldest daughter, as if about to burst with pride. Which they were indeed entitled to do, having had it hard throughout the dark 'post-Daddy' years with every penny counting and each scrap of bread and bit of fish gathered up to go into the next day's dinner. But they had managed. With the help of the most wonderful neighbours a family had ever known and the strength that God had given them, they had endured, thought Mrs Tiernan. And now her daughter was to be a nurse! Small tears came into her eyes as she thought of her eldest daughter, resplendent now in her spanking new uniform, standing in a vast, polished ward, surrounded by awe-stricken colleagues. Her fist closed as, unbidden, vague folk memories of coffin ships and starving wretches pawing the stench-ridden dark came to her, and suddenly she felt limitlessly empowered. It was all she could do not to cry out, 'My daughter's going to be a nurse! Ha ha! Ha ha ha ha!', clutch the sweeping brush, which was very close to hand, and proceed around the kitchen with triumphant, almost girlish glee.

But she didn't. Dignity and restraint won the day and all she did as she reposed in a single funnel of dusty sunlight was bite her lower lip and softly intone the words: 'God be praised for sending us, his loyal servants, the Tiernans of Barntrosna village, such happiness true and bountiful.'

Rarely in her life had Mrs Tiernan known such feelings. Or her daughter Noreen now as she took her seat in the neat and tidy compartment of the British Rail train which was about to make its way steadily all the way from Holyhead to Euston Station, London. Outside, fields and hills sped by. Fields and hills and sheep – English sheep! The first, she reflected, she had ever seen. There were butterflies in Noreen's tummy as she thought now of all the exciting days that lay ahead of her. The moment she arrived, she would write home and tell them all about it. She had promised Ta that she would send him a special postcard. How she was going to miss him! And Bimbo! But, as she had told them, she would be back at Christmas when the fields were covered in a white eiderdown of snow – and the tales she would have for them then!

Of course, it had been especially hard saying goodbye to Pobs (her pet name for her boyfriend) – how would it not be when she loved him so dearly? As he did her, revealing the true depth of his feeling when he broke down in tears in the dance hall, crying: 'No! No! Don't go to England! They'll take you away from me just like they took everything else!'

He was such a good sort, Pobs. Emotional, yes, but as kind and considerate a boy as any girl could ever wish for. She had promised she would write every day. 'You promise?' Pobs had implored, wiping his eyes with the large white handkerchief which he seemed to bring everywhere with him. 'I promise,' Noreen had replied, and despite the fact that things did not quite turn out like that, her sincerity at the time was unquestionable.

*

The backs of houses sped by as she thought of St Bartholomew's; what would it be like, she wondered. No, she didn't wonder. Didn't, because she *knew*! Knew that within its walls there would be beautifully polished corridors and nurses with watches pinned to their starched uniforms and preoccupied young doctors running around with clipboards, vases of roses neatly placed on tables at various intervals throughout the wards – and of course, patients.

But, most of all, a children's ward. How she hoped she was assigned there on her 'probby' (as the girls called their six months' probation). Which she knew because Imelda Stronge, who was now a fully qualified nurse in Huddersfield, had told her so. They had had a lovely few drinks in the Arms Hotel before Imelda returned. 'Always remember to call it that now, Noreen,' she had instructed her, 'Won't you? Probby, I mean!'

'Yes,' Noreen had dutifully replied, 'probby.'

*

Armed with this knowledge, Noreen felt a confidence building quietly within her as the train sped along, a conviction that there would be few challenges in the coming days which she would be incapable of facing. A billboard, SUPPORT THE NHS, sped past and Noreen smiled. She thought of herself sitting there, on the edge of a small bed, reading from *Tommy the Turtle* or *My Friend Alpaca* with all the children ranged around her, gazing up adoringly. A tiny tremor of satisfaction ran through her.

That was not to say, she realized, that there wouldn't be hard work too – of course there would! And nobody knew it better than Noreen! But she was more than prepared for it, and would see to it that through a combination of the fiercest effort and the intercession of St Jude – who was the saint to whom she had the deepest devotion – she would come through her first-year exams with flying colours.

As indeed she might have, if only – almost as soon as she arrived at St Bartholomew's – things had not begun to go horribly wrong, a chain of events being set in motion which would ultimately not only result in Mrs Tiernan abandoning her perfectly contented life as a Barntrosna housewife for one of obsessed and dedicated private detection, but propel a perfectly ordinary, God-fearing, truly conscientious young nurse to the very brink of death and destruction.

*

It was 4.05 p.m. and Noreen, standing with her belted suitcase at her knee, was in such a state of excitement that she was not entirely aware of what was going on around her, to such an extent that when the sister superior (a potato-shaped woman in her forties) placed her hands on her shoulders and exclaimed: 'Noreen! There you are! I'm going to take you over to the Nurses' Home where you'll be billeted for the entire duration of your stay with us!' Noreen heard the involuntary ejaculation of 'Omigod!' leaping from her lips in a tiny squeal!

How her head swirled as she followed the older woman along the corridor, a succession of blurred portraits of long-dead philanthropists and mutton-chopped physicians assailing her with bewildering rapidity – but excitingly so! The alabaster statue of a little boy, representing the victims of a Victorian cholera epidemic, seemed to salute her with his outstretched hand and cry out: 'Welcome to St Bartholomew's, Noreen!'

As their heels clicked on the brilliantly polished black and white tiles, Noreen Tiernan sighed anew. She touched her forehead gently in an effort to stay the whooshing, planet-like rotations that were assailing her consciousness at that moment. Then, as the sister superior led her into the building through the door which bore the nameplate NURSES' HOME, Noreen almost fainted – because of the realization that at last she was here – in St Bartholomew's! In England!

*

It is possible, without a doubt, to consider, in retrospect, what might have transpired if A wing had been their destination on that particular occasion – and not the fatal B wing, the stairs of which she was now briskly ascending with her officious, astoundingly spotless companion. Because, of course, in the former, where the students spent the greater proportion of their free time locating imaginary epidermal imperfections (principally in the regions of the face and neck), obsessively bathing feet and driving themselves to distraction with seemingly interminable combinations of apparel – nowhere was there to be found a student who responded to the name 'Sticky' (Stephanie) Diggs. Who, although she could not have possibly known it at the time, of course, was destined to become what can only truthfully be called – Noreen Tiernan's nemesis!

*

Idle speculation is, of course, of little value now, and all that need concern us here is the indisputable fact that it was firmly within the four walls of B wing that Noreen Tiernan now found herself, being – with something of a giddy flourish, indeed, uncharacteristic as it might seem – introduced with the words: 'Stephanie – I want you to meet Noreen Tiernan. She's to be your room mate for the next year!'

Perhaps if the sister superior, or indeed Noreen, had been possessed of finely tuned, highly intuitive powers such as might be encountered in the pages of light fiction or the average daytime television crime series, they might instinctively have attributed some measure of significance to the fact that the pink pointed tip of Stephanie's tongue (for all the world like the smallest fleshy arrowhead) was protruding ever so slightly from between her lips and was literally quivering as her eyes locked onto the figure of Noreen Tiernan with an intensity that was quite startling, especially when her gaze exhibited no sign of flinching, her eyes – like two tiny twin cameras – inspecting Noreen's lengthy, flowing tresses, blooming pink cheeks, and, of course, the soft heaving slopes of her bosom as she extended her hand and flushed crimson, shyly uttering the words: 'Hello, I'm Noreen.'

*

Of great significance at this meeting was the vast difference in presentation which announced itself instantly between Noreen and her room mate to be. For, whereas Noreen's hair was soft

173

and feminine, spilling onto her shoulders in waves of molten copper, Stephanie's – what little she had of it! – resembled nothing so much as a clump of the coarsest mountain gorse. Noteworthy too was the difference between their noses – it seemed as if, while Noreen's was small, perfectly and elegantly contoured, Stephanie's was a weathered, bulbous affair not unlike a species of root vegetable. Their taste in clothes, too, seemed to indicate between them an abyss of unbridgeable proportions. Noreen's delicately billowing cottons and forget-me-not patterned silks were nothing if not light-years away from Stephanie's 'County Home Trousers', as her father might have referred to them, above the waistband of which it was possible – breathtaking in its ostentation, indeed! – to make out the stitched brand-name of a company whose supremacy in the marketplace was a consequence of unrivalled excellence in the manufacture of men's underpants – *Healthex*!

*

As for the hospital, however, Noreen loved it more than she could have dared to dream! Especially since she had been assigned to the children's ward, reading aloud with all her heart to the little sick mites as they returned from toileting each morning. How she looked forward to those mornings now! Barely be able to contain herself as she bade goodbye to 'Stef' (as she now instinctively called her!) and clacked across the polished corridors with her books tucked under her arm, unconsciously rehearsing the speech which she habitually made each morning before she bent her russet head to read. 'Very well, children! Now that we've done all our poos, I want you all to sit up straight and listen to Tommy the Turtle! Arms folded, now!'

All the kiddies loved Tommy. Especially when he went to

the city to meet Tara Turtle. They loved that, all scrunching up their noses as they laughed into their hands. 'O Tommy!' Noreen used to say when he kissed Tara. 'Tommy! You naughty turtle!' It was the best fun ever in the hospital!

*

It was upon her return to A wing from one of these sessions on a Thursday morning in early September 1980 that Noreen looked up and saw Nurse Jennifer Hayes coming walking towards her with her arms swinging. Nurse Hayes was nice but she was a tad old fashioned and set in her ways. As all the girls said: 'O, Hayesy's all right but she's been here for yonks!' And truly it was hard not to laugh when you saw her in her old flat shoes and big chunky cardigan. As Noreen observed to Stephanie: 'She reminds me of what I would have been like if I'd stayed in Barntrosna, Stef! A big country galoot!'

Which is, in terms of this narrative, a truly telling remark. Especially considering the lack of restraint with which it was delivered. After all, it must be remembered that for most of her life Noreen Tiernan had been a dutiful, exemplary Barntrosna girl, fiercely – if quietly – loyal to both family, friends and fellow citizens of the town.

And now, here she was, inexplicably insulting the place of her birth with the brazen implication that to remain there beyond a certain length of time was to risk a certain 'unfashionability'. It was not the only odd remark made by Noreen Tiernan around this time; soon there were to be many others.

*

For it is useless to pretend that she was the same girl now who had arrived at the hospital only some few short weeks before. How much exactly was her own fault and to what degree she might present a case for mitigation shall always be a matter of conjecture. What was certain was that now the clock had been set ticking and there could be no going back. The girl who had once been 'the old Noreen Tiernan' would never have wantonly flung her pencil from her and caustically snapped: 'Oh, I'm fed up writing this! What's the use of writing to Pobs every night! It's stupid!'

Perhaps – in an extreme situation of almost unbearable tiredness and confusion occasioned by excessive demands on the wards – the words might have regrettably passed her lips.

But such was not the case. As she sat at the table with her writing materials on its surface before her, those words had only one meaning and one alone – that an unbridgeable fissure had opened up in the relationship between her and Pobs McCue. Had Noreen, in that first instant whereupon those hasty, injudicious words had been uttered by her, placed at her elbow a small mirror, she would have been witness to a quiet, unspectacular development which was soon to prove of the utmost significance – for already a sly smile, as thin as wire, was making its way across the face of Stephanie 'Sticky' Diggs, who was sitting directly behind her in the rattan chair (purchased, not insignificantly, in the back streets of a Bangkok market!) with her bared legs thrown rakishly over its curved edges, inhaling the smoke from a slender cheroot. Sadly, however, no such mirror was in evidence that night, and thus events continued apace.

*

It was some days later that Noreen Tiernan found herself standing in the main corridor of St Bartholomew's hospital, with the sister superior (who, she had learned, because of her

excess weight the students had uncharitably named 'Tank')
breezily enquiring after her mother's welfare and quizzing her
repeatedly as to how she liked London. And who – quite out
of nowhere – suddenly gripped her fiercely by the arm and
forced her – how else can you describe it? – into a corner
demanding to know how *Miss Diggs* was *behaving herself.*

Noreen felt certain there must be black and blue marks
appearing on her upper arm as the older nurse breathlessly
continued: 'You must tell me! Have you had any – *trouble* with
her?'

At this point, Noreen Tiernan found herself at a loss for
words. O for heaven's sake, what is the old fool on about? she
asked herself. She was beginning to understand now why all
the girls made a laugh of her. ('I see Tank is wearing a lovely
top today!' she would often hear them scorn, indulging in
pseudo-laudatory dialogues concerning her shoes and hairstyle
when they were not drawing pictures of her in their lecture
folders, colouring in great big beards on her rotund form in
brown felt marker.) Which was why she sighed and thought to
herself: I wish she would leave me alone and go about her
business, the old heifer! But she did not give any indication of
this as she replied: 'No – no trouble. No trouble at all, Sister.
She's a lovely girl.' She endeavoured to be as mannerly as she
could, hoping to 'shift the hairy old gasbag' – as she was now
in her own mind referring to her. Which at last transpired but
not before her arm was squeezed one more time and she
found herself wincing as – almost hopefully – the older nurse
growled: 'Don't forget! I'm always here if you need me! And
remember – there's nothing I haven't heard before! If she lays
a finger on you . . .'

At which point the sister superior broke off, a high-ranking rival appearing suddenly at the end of the lime-green corridor like a startled cabbage white on a stalk.

*

When Stephanie heard this story, she nearly, as she said herself, went and 'wet her farking pants!' 'Why, the old dingbat!' she chortled, puffing on a cheroot. 'Can you believe that cheeky cah?'

In truth, Noreen couldn't believe it but what she could believe was what her room mate said some moments later, her eyes lighting up flirtatiously: 'I'll bet you'll never guess where I've been!' Noreen was a little bit nervous because of course she still had a long way to go before she was a real, uninhibited London 'gel' like Stef. But she approximated as best she could and, contriving herself to be chewing a stick of heavily minted gum, replied: 'No! Where, Stef?'

Stephanie's eyes glittered with excitement. 'Da-dan!' she cried, and out of nowhere a star leapt off shining glass. Astonished, Noreen found herself staring straight at a gleaming bottle of full-strength undiluted Russian vodka!

There are those indeed who would argue that what occurred on that fateful night was not in any sense a crime at all. This, however – as was subsequently proven to be the case – would not have been the view of Fr Luke Doody, Pobs McCue, Mrs Tiernan herself – or, most likely, *any* of the townspeople of Barntrosna. Which Noreen would have known instinctively, of course, but by the time she had consumed a substantial quantity of the aforementioned vodka, she really did not care an awful lot what their views might be – not only on that particular subject but, quite simply, on any at all! Which was why, when Stephanie quipped mischievously: 'I bet you're wearing your black one tonight, aren't you,

178

Noreen?' that she chuckled and cheekily scooped up her sweater, revealing her white lacy brassière with the little rosebud nestled in between the cups, and with an unbridled howl of mirth fell backwards onto the bed with her white-stockinged legs giddily, furiously, scything the air. Quite how Stephanie managed to manoeuvre herself into the position she did, in retrospect seems quite remarkable. But it proved to be devastatingly effective, for before the Barntrosna girl could even begin to know what was happening, her room mate's lips had welded themselves to hers and she found herself barely able to breathe. The young nurse blanched. It suddenly seemed absurd that such a thing could be occurring. She considered that it was a kind of game. A Nurses' Home initiation ceremony, perhaps? But – how could it be? After all, she had been in the hospital for months! What then was it? Noreen Tiernan's mind whirled. Then, out of nowhere, she felt the pincer jaws of guilt and fear tightening at the base of her spine. Perspiration beads squeezed their way to her brow as she writhed frantically in an effort to wrench herself free. 'No!' snapped Stephanie angrily. There could be no doubting the firmness of the admonition. 'No!' she repeated and glared at her prone, exhausted colleague. As the strength ebbed from her limbs, Noreen Tiernan summoned what resources were at her disposal and weakly cried: 'Stef! Let me up! Let me up, please!'

But it was clear from the expression on Stephanie Diggs' face that she had no intention of doing any such thing! In that instant, Noreen Tiernan thought of Pobs, the tears flowing down the front of his jacket as he howled: 'How could you, Noreen? How could you!' She thought of her mother, her knees practically worn away to nothing as she stormed Heaven for guidance. She thought of Nabs Brennan, scratching his head and murmuring perplexedly: 'A tragedy! That's all you can call it! Thank God himself is in the grave!' and she thought of Fr Doody as he thumped the pulpit and barked: 'It is forbidden by the law of God! You hear me? Your rancid body will burn in the pit of hell, Tiernan, for what you've done!'

What occurred directly after that is not entirely clear. That Stephanie administered some kind of drug would seem to be beyond question. For, try as she might, somewhere behind the vague and swirling smoky haze that was her mind Noreen Tiernan could not bring herself to resist as once more she heard herself darkly instructed to 'Kiss me, slave!', the tongue of Stephanie Diggs probing wickedly, brooking no resistance. Eventually, triumphantly, crying: 'That wasn't so bad, was it?' as, to her delight, she perceived Noreen's arm curling about her waist and her own body being drawn slowly downwards until, in a mélange of deliriously indulgent falsetto cries, they were as one.

*

When Noreen awoke the next morning, she felt as though she had been pounded incessantly over the head with a blunt if not series of blunt instruments. She stared in shame at the stuffed ashtray, her bagged stockings. She turned her head away and instantly wanted to be sick. She found herself consumed by a desire to rush to the chapel and beg forgiveness. She started as a familiar, but oddly deeper, voice snapped: 'Get me my robe, nah!' and her heart missed a beat as it dawned on her that Stephanie had not in fact departed but had been right beside her all along – standing in the shower! A tiny nerve trembled in Noreen's cheek as she sat on the edge of the bed. Part of her wanted to cry out: 'No! I won't get you your robe! You're filthy! Filthy and horrible and I despise you! Tank was right! Oh, God! Why didn't I listen to her when she warned me about you!'

It seems perplexing now that another part of Noreen Tiernan was jockeying for position – unless, of course, we attribute such a development to the last vestiges of the drug which were as yet coursing within her – and brazenly suggesting that she make a completely different reply, to wit: 'Why yes, darling! But of course I will, Diggsy, sweetest!'

Which – unbelievably! – was the response she eventually made, her voice delightedly quivering and her legs turning to jelly as she trembled beneath the taller girl who, vigorously drying her hair, fixed her with her by now familiar piercing gaze and demanded to know: 'Well! And how are you feeling this morning, you tasty thing, you?'

'Fine, Diggsy,' came the weak-willed answer, the only one Noreen felt capable of giving. The older (Stephanie was approaching twenty) nurse's reply was harsh and immediate. 'Fine? Fine! Is that all you can say?'

Noreen reddened deeply and looked away. She wished the cheaply carpeted floor of the pungently odorous room would open up and swallow her.

A thin smile undulated across Stephanie Diggs' lips, accompanied by the tiniest of chortles.

'So! Going all coy now, are we? So that's the game, is it, Tiernan! Let's face it, honey! You loved it! Couldn't get enough, could you? Ha ha!'

Noreen felt as if her cheeks were about to sprout flame. Then, suddenly, her heart leaped. The older girl was coming towards her! She felt her chin gripped by hard, tobacco-stained fingers (Stephanie thought nothing of going through three packs a day) as she heard the words:

'You did, didn't you, chicken? Tell me! I want you to tell me! I want to hear you say it!'

'I loved it, Stef!' Noreen was astonished to hear herself cry, her swivelling eyeballs the size of the brass knobs on the bedstead.

'Damn right!' leered Diggsy, her hand moving slowly towards the nylon-clad uplands of Noreen's bottom. 'Now – get out there and make me my breakfast!'

In that instant, Noreen Tiernan's mind whirled and a thousand questions went racing through her mind: What had happened? How could she have allowed herself to be drugged? The word *breakfast* seemed to appear before her in giant Day-Glo letters, followed closely by neonscape video logos that read: '*Breakfast! Breakfast!*' Why had she left Barntrosna, she asked herself over and over again, Barntrosna where resided Pobs, her beautiful kind and gentle lover? Left it all to find herself trapped in this hellhole with this . . . this . . .

Tears rolled down her cheeks like twin rivers.

*

At the end of the bed Stephanie lit a cigarette. Noreen became aware that she was glaring at her in the most hostile manner. 'Are you going to sit there all day, huh? Huh, cherry?' she barked suddenly. 'Are you? Get up off your country ass and fix that breakfast!'

The cruel words bit deep into Noreen as she dropped her eyes and staggered shamefully to the kitchenette in a half-daze.

*

Of course, in the days that followed, to Noreen's fellow students everything proceeded as normal, and if you had taken any of them aside and said: 'Do you realize Noreen Tiernan is embroiled in a perversely impassioned love affair with Stephanie Diggs of B wing?', they would have had no compunction about telling you you were out of your mind. All except perhaps for sister superior, Tank, who had harboured suspicions all along but had never at any time been in possession of the slightest shred of evidence with which to back them up. After all, what was out of the ordinary about two young girls dressing up and going out on a Friday night to enjoy some well-earned relaxation? Nothing in the slightest except that, of course, in this case, the discotheque in question was called Madame Pork's and was located in a dimly lit basement in Soho, not to mention almost exclusively patronized by women who were attracted to members of their own sex. Not only that, indeed, but were particularly attracted to the idea of using physical violence on them and bossing them around if they didn't do what they were told. One wonders what the staff nurses who maternally folded their arms and remarked good-naturedly, 'There's the girls – off to enjoy themselves again!' whenever they saw Noreen and Stephanie leaving by the front gates might have made of that, not to mention such little details as the intricacy of the chain-link harness that Stephanie had of late begun to insist that Noreen wear beneath her clothes – even when she was at work! 'But I can't wear those!' Noreen had initially protested. 'They stick into me, Stef!'

'Shut up, Tiernan!' had been the terse response. 'You'll wear it and like it!'

'At least let me take it off when I'm on the ward!' Noreen had begged.

But Stephanie Diggs had allowed her no quarter.

'If you don't do what I say, I'll finish with you!' had been her cold-hearted, uncompromising stricture.

There were times now when Noreen began to feel so despondent that it might in fact be more accurate to say that she was consumed by despair. More than once the taking of her own life had seemed an inviting option. But then, oddly, and for no apparent reason whatsoever, her spirits would lift quite unexpectedly and she would find herself looking forward to Stephanie's return from the wards – becoming somewhat light-headed and girlish at the prospect, in fact! – as she sat there waiting for the moment when she would be called upon to fall to the floor and remove her room mate's white shoes, at all times referring to her as 'Miss'. If she did not comply with this latter instruction (a recent innovation) she received a firm smack, along with a curt denunciation along the lines of: 'Maybe that might put manners on you, you cheeky little strap, you!'

Who can say what tenebrous arteries one might find winding their way in those mysterious caverns that lurk beneath that cheerfully oblivious main highway that is life? Surely anyone in their right mind would have gone straight to the hospital authorities – if not the police indeed! – and firmly made their case by insisting: 'This has gone far enough! I refuse to be manhandled and abused in this manner any longer!'

Even have gone so far, perhaps, as to cry aloud: 'This is harassment!' and who knows, receive some compensation from the college as a result.

In the labyrinthine core of her being, somewhere, there most definitely was a part of Noreen Tiernan that dearly longed to take this course of action. But it was not to be. And for that – perplexing as it might be for those of us who do not fully comprehend the intricate workings of the human soul *in extremis*! – there was but one reason and one reason alone –

Noreen Tiernan was fabulously, hopelessly, in love. For, for every pert smack and 'Damn you, Tiernan!' that she received (not to mention any number of 'Look at you, you lazy little slut's), there was forever burning within her the tiny flame of hope that once again would be repeated another of those special, tender moments when Stephanie would take her in her arms – quite out of the blue on some occasions! – stroke her hair and whisper mischievously into her ear: 'Who's my favourite little nurse?' Which would, when it happened, miraculously transform those prickly moments which had become part of their lives into so many heart-lifting soap bubbles blown away for ever by a light and airy breeze.

And so life proceeded. Bedpans and thermometers all week, Madame Pork's each Friday without fail and a great big breakfast in bed for Stephanie every Saturday morning. To us, odd, without a doubt, but nonetheless it still cannot be denied that the growing relationship between Noreen and Stephanie had already begun to work better than did those of many what we prefer to call 'normal' people. Such, in fact, was the bond that had formed between them that Noreen would often buy little presents for her lover and, along with small perfumed flower-bordered notes, leave them where she knew they would be discovered. True, there were still occasional difficulties between them – Noreen was, even yet, prone to sobbing fits, just as Stephanie was to hysterical outbursts of rage, during which she would assault Noreen long and hard with her fists, calling her all sorts of names, including 'Bog-face!' and 'Bucket feet!', which stung her – unsurprisingly – right to the very core of her being. Incredible as it may seem, the older nurse had on one occasion stooped so low as to rasp, 'Lappy lugs,' causing Noreen to erupt once more in floods of tears.

It seems incomprehensible that such a liaison ought to have

prospered in the slightest. But prosper it did, albeit in its own idiosyncratic oblique fashion – the bond that, despite everything, they had managed to fashion between them strengthening with every day that passed.

Many of which had already sped by, at a furious rate of knots indeed, and before she knew it Noreen had been almost thirteen months in St Bartholomew's General Hospital, Chiswick. Which absolutely amazed her, for never before had she known time to pass with such rapidity, as she remarked to Stephanie on one occasion when they were preparing for a wild night in Madame Pork's. 'God, Stef,' (she employed the affectionate diminutive at all times now), she sighed, adjusting the links of her harness beneath her armpit, 'I really don't know where the time has gone! To think that it's really a whole year and a month since I came to St Barty's.'

For the unassailable truth was that – bewildering as it might seem – after exactly thirteen months since that day when she had waved goodbye to all her friends at Barntrosna Station, Noreen Tiernan had never been happier. There was even talk, it soon emerged, of her winning the much-coveted Nurse of the Year prize! No doubt how this will come as a great surprise to the average reader. But the explanation for it all really is quite simple. Stephanie Diggs had completely and utterly swept the young girl off her feet – and where, once upon a time, Noreen might have shyly retreated from her advances with mild protests such as 'Oh no! I don't want to do that!' or 'What? Put *that* in *there*? You can't be serious!' she now yelped: 'Yes!' and 'Oh but yes!' and was so exultant as a consequence that the quality of her work on the wards was regarded as second to none.

Events, however, were to take a more puzzling turn when,

some months on, it was Stephanie who began to make the mild protests, trying to fabricate an excuse every time that 'look' came into Noreen's eye or she licked her lips lasciviously as she said: 'Are you by any chance playing hard to get, Steffy Diggs? I hope honeybuns is not playing hard to get now, is she?'

Whereupon the two of them would launch into it once more – 'hammer and tongs' – with blouse buttons flying, pinging musically against the rims of mirrors and oval-framed snapshots of Noreen's home town.

The casual mention of which brings us back to that tranquil corner of the earth, which Noreen Tiernan had for so long called home, prior to her fatal departure for foreign shores and the hospital called St Bartholomew's.

Now there are some uncharitable folk who, if you were to enquire of them as to their opinion of this particular piece of God's little acre, might shock you with the cold-blooded, insensitive nature of their replies. Which might possibly be something along the lines of: 'Barntrosna? Don't talk to me about that dump! A one-horse town and the horse has croaked it!' or, 'Barntrosna? If God put a more godforsaken outdoor lunatic asylum on this earth when He was going about His business making it, then I am afraid nobody has ever bothered to tell me about it!'

A view with which Pobs McCue would no doubt concur, having for the first three months after Noreen's departure and the gradually discontinued missives managed to put a brave face on it, cheerily quipping, 'Ah, sure, she's too busy to be writing. Them auld exams they give them at the nursing – they're fierce hard!' and continuing to do so until he could bear it no longer, one night in the Bridge Bar bursting out, wild-eyed: 'What are youse all looking at me for! Do youse think I care if she wrote no letter to me? I can get any amount of women! Any amount, youse fuckers, youse!'

Some people took a dim view of his behaviour on this occasion and remarked that it might be a good idea if Pobs McCue learned some manners for himself. But there were others present who not only empathized with him but understood his anxieties at a very profound level.

*

One of these was Eustace De Vere-Bingham, a quiet and reserved good-natured man who had devoted his entire life to the study of exotic flora and fauna, whiling away his daily hours in the study of De Vere-Bingham Hall, a magnificently constructed Palladian edifice on the edge of Barntrosna, when he wasn't cruising merrily up and down the country lanes in his cherry-red bubble car, while all the country folk appeared at the doors of their cottages crying hoarsely: 'Look! It's the Protestant in his motor car!'

Eustace had come to know Noreen quite well over the years – she had been something of a 'little Catholic pet' in the De Vere-Bingham mansion, his mother often observing: 'The little face of her! Charming soul!' when she appeared at the back door in her wellington boots, sucking her fingers – and was troubled and deeply puzzled by the fact that no one had heard anything from her, particularly Pobs, who was a long-standing drinking partner of his. As he sat in the lounge of the Bridge nursing his gin and tonic, the sheer enormity of the situation suddenly seemed to hit him. The skin beneath his signet ring paled as his fingers closed around the glass and the erratic canals along his brow straightened themselves with lightning precision. 'Something has to be done – *must* be done!

Otherwise Pobs shall go off his head! I'm sure of it!' were the words he murmured to himself as he fixed his gaze on the yellowing calendar in front of him. He resolved at once to call on Noreen's mother the following day and, as he unlocked his car door and adjusted his Harris tweed plus-fours, through gritted teeth, continued: 'And find out, once and for all, just what the hell is going on!'

But, as Eustace was soon to discover, to his deepening consternation, Mrs Tiernan knew almost as little about the situation as himself. Was practically beside herself with worry, in fact.

*

Perhaps one of the most curious and fascinating aspects of village life as it is lived in Ireland is its seemingly uncomplicated 'code of behaviour'; the inhabitants of any village are, at any time, assumed to live simple, dutiful, perhaps even predictable lives, with clearly defined social and moral parameters. Expectations are generally low, with people going about their business much as their antecedents did hundreds of years before. So established are the rhythmic patterns of behaviour in such places that any radical departures from them are considered to be quite unthinkable. But how close is this to the truth, or is it but a chimera – behind the innocent façade lurking a reality as shocking as any seething mass of serpents uncovered by two arms sunk deep in a barrel of seemingly fragrant, beguiling pot-pourri? In Barntrosna's case, as later events would soon reveal, this was indeed the sad and challenging actuality.

*

At this stage in our narrative, it is important that we return to Noreen's mother, who by now was at her wits' end. Endless communications to her daughter had produced nothing. Fevered night dreams in which Noreen was brutally assaulted, dumped over cliffs and leered at by Bill Sykes-featured assailants had by now become commonplace. For the first time in her life, Mrs Tiernan found herself helpless. She would sit alone in the gloom of the stone-flagged kitchen, biting her nails and thinking over the many tribulations and small crises she had overcome during the course of her life: the death of her dear husband; the time her sister (Ellie) had the sciatica; the eighteen hours she had spent in the labour ward with Noreen; all were as nothing compared to this. Perhaps if Noreen had even been a tad unreliable in her habits, Mrs Tiernan might have understood. But this was not the case. The words of Mrs Donnelly came racing into her mind, those very words she had uttered thirteen months before on being informed that Noreen had been offered a nursing position in London: 'Don't let her go, Mrs! If you let her go near it, you'll regret it until your dying day! Listen to me now for the love of God! Tramps, whoremasters, madmen, the whole lot of them! Every low form of life that God put on this earth is to be found there – waiting for the likes of you and me! Waiting for her – Noreen! Your daughter!'

She wondered now, had Mrs Donnelly been right all along? No! She couldn't be! There was some other rational explanation! All she had to do was wait a few more days and a reply would most definitely arrive, explaining everything.

But no letter ever came. It was only after meeting Pobs, whom she encountered outside the butcher's shop in tears, that she decided once and for all it was time to act. 'What are we going to do?' cried Pobs as he pulled at her coat. Mrs Tiernan sighed and her eyes too moistened. She could not bear to look upon him suffering so. 'There, there,' she said and handed him a rolled-up Kleenex tissue she had in her handbag. Perhaps if Eustace De Vere-Bingham had not been on his way home from the Bridge Bar at that moment events might never have acquired the momentum that they did. For when he perceived the advanced state of Pobs's despair, he was truly incensed. 'Dear God,' he cried, 'nobody should have to endure such pain! It is an obscenity!'

'I'm at my wits' end, Eustace,' Mrs Tiernan blurted out, 'and that's the truth! In all the time that she's been away, not so much as a card or a letter or a phone call!'

*

Now, the idea of Mrs Tiernan becoming an 'investigator' leading a party of self-styled 'fact-finders' to the great city of London in order to ascertain what has happened to a missing daughter is in itself inherently ridiculous. Of course it is! One can't but be aware of that! For whatever about well-bred, tweed-skirted post-war English ladies becoming world-renowned sleuths, Mrs Tiernan knew she was no Miss Marple! Had never – ever! – at any time in her life entertained such extravagant notions about herself! She knew better, for heaven's sake. She was a simple, God-fearing woman of humble origins and if she decided to take this burden upon herself, it was for one reason and one reason alone – to locate the daughter she dearly loved. Selfish ambition had nothing to do with it!

No, Mrs Tiernan was not and most definitely did not see herself as an investigator in the Kojak or Columbo mould, or indeed any other representation of the profession as might be encountered daily on the television or in the pages of cheap pulp thrillers.

No, she was just an ordinary woman doing a mother's duty.

Something, as she often remarked many months later when it was all over, she could never have done – not in a million years – without the help of her friends and fellow villagers. Chief among them being Pobs, Eustace De Vere-Bingham and, of course, Fr Luke.

*

It was only a matter of time, of course – such had been the level of murmurings and disquieted exchanges amongst his parishioners – before Fr Luke determined that something was indeed seriously amiss in the locality and why, when he met Pobs on the road some days later, he had this to say to him: 'Well, Pobs – are you going to let me in on the little secret? Just what is going on around here, eh? It's something to do with Noreen, isn't it?'

'Yes,' replied Pobs, lowering his head for a brief moment as the toe of his hobnailed boot described a variety of random shapes on the gravel beneath it, then raising it once more to say: 'We think she may have been kidnapped.'

'Kidnapped, you say?' exclaimed the clergyman as a blue tit on the sycamore directly behind him suddenly took wing, as if in fright.

Pobs nodded gravely.

*

When the full story was revealed to him, Fr Luke was adamant. 'No! I refuse to stand idly by, Pobs! She is my parishioner, after all!'

Pobs placed the nicotine-stained nail of one thumb under the other and flicked for a moment. 'Do you understand, Pobs?' his parish priest demanded, squeezing his shoulder with an enormous weather-beaten hand.

'Yes,' Pobs replied softly.

'Right so! Leave it with me, then, Pobs!' he heard then and looked up to see Fr Luke already making his way up the hill to the presbytery with his shiny-patched soutane flapping excitedly, expectantly behind him like the wings of a giant bat.

*

Eustace De Vere-Bingham loved butterflies. There wasn't a butterfly in the world he hadn't caught at some point. There was nothing surprising about the sight of the only De Vere-Bingham left in the Big House (De Vere-Bingham Hall) chasing across the fields with a butterfly net, in pursuit of some powder-winged beauty wantonly disporting itself about the firmament, with a dazzlingly teasing display of so many figure-eights. Some people disliked Eustace. 'Him and that fucking bubble car of his,' they would mumble, 'he'd sicken your effing arse!' To see him roaring into the village in the cherry-red conveyance, seemingly under the impression that he was some sort of world-class rally driver, insensitively calling out to garage mechanics and grocery assistants alike, 'Fill her up like a good fellow!' and 'Have you my goodies ready, fine chap?' had the effect of affronting them as he spurted off in a cloud of foul-smelling smoke to entertain yet another group of 'friends' with a salacious selection of his so-called 'nudie-cuties'. (His latest acquisition being *Back Street Jane – The Ben Hur of Big Titty Movies!*) 'Effing bollocks,' it was often said of him, 'a good kick in the hole would take care of him and his dirty films!'

But that is not to say that Eustace De Vere-Bingham was entirely without friends. Fr Luke, for one, was his champion, and would not hear a word said against him. 'What of it, if he collects butterflies? Is that to be considered a crime? Not in the eyes of God, my friends – and you would do well to remember that! Let him who is without sin cast the first stone!'

For, after all, the priest would continue, Eustace was an example, in many ways. To begin with, he was honest. Law-abiding too. When was the last time you heard of *him* breaking into the Bridge Bar to avail himself of crates of ale and any number of cigarettes? Or threatening to break every window in Barntrosna, and suchlike? Not for him nonsensical late-night political debates outside the Burger Hut, when over some farcical detail an innocent citizen could find him- or herself kicked up and down the length of the main street and every member of their family – despite total lack of involvement – remorselessly insulted.

Which was why, at precisely eight o'clock on the night after Fr Luke had taken his leave of Pobs, a knock came to the once-magnificent oaken door of De Vere-Bingham Hall.

*

'London, you say?' repeated Eustace De Vere as he cradled his cut-glass tumbler of French brandy and stared grimly through the south-facing window that looked out upon the row of silver birches his great-grandfather had planted years before. 'Noreen – whom we adored all the years she spent coming to visit us here in this house!'

'Yes,' replied the priest, sipping his tea from a hand-painted china cup, discreetly averting his eyes from the podgy white limbs of the interlocking oriental figures who cavorted beneath its rim with abandon.

Eustace De Vere-Bingham turned to face his visitor. It was clear that he could have been startlingly handsome but for two alarmingly prominent teeth and a recalcitrant corkscrew-shaped wave of sandy-coloured hair. He stood six foot two in his Norfolk jacket and brown shoes.

'I would not have come to you unless I considered it to be a matter of utmost importance,' said Fr Luke.

'I realize that,' replied Eustace, emptying the contents of his glass with one swift gulp and almost immediately replenishing it.

There was a long pause. Outside a man went running by, pausing only to wave.

'I see Turbie has escaped from Our Lady of Lourdes Mental Hospital again,' said Fr Luke, not without a tinge of regret.

Eustace did not reply. He was deep in thought. The grandfather clock in the corner ticked like a gigantic watch, each second passing like a solid blow to the solar plexus. The priest stared at the remainder of his tea. It made the shape of a small brown dog, with a tail and three little legs.

'Well, Eustace,' he said then, the sudden movement of his hand demolishing the tiny liquid canine as that of a malign deity might some degenerate city, 'can I count you in?'

The smile began at the corner of the Protestant landowner's mouth and, within seconds, was stretched right across the lower half of his face. He raised his right arm and pointed with his index finger, indicating the large flower bed in the south-eastern corner of the garden.

'Do you see those gladioli?' he said.

The priest nodded.

'It was Noreen's father planted them,' said Eustace, grimly but steadfastly.

'I can count you in, then?' cried the clergyman eagerly.

Eustace nodded, uttering only one word as he placed his fastidiously manicured hand on the smiling priest's shoulder.

That word was: 'Yes.'

*

The big day came, and Mrs Tiernan's tummy was a-flutter, principally because she hadn't been to London since that one and only time with her dear departed husband Oweny James thirty years before. What would it be like, she wondered. Just then, her thoughts were interrupted by a sudden cry of: 'Don't think you'll tell me what to do, De Vere! You've been doing that for long enough! You and all belonging to you!' Instinctively, Noreen's mother climbed out of the minibus and pleaded with the two men – Eustace De Vere-Bingham and Pobs – who despite never having, up until now, ever so much as exchanged a cross word – they were long-standing drinking partners, for Heaven's sake! – were already grappling vigorously with one another, a state of affairs perhaps occasioned by the heightened state of nervous tension and anticipation which their imminent journey to the English metropolis engendered within them. Mrs Tiernan had never actually come between two grown men before but she knew that if she did not unequivocally display strength and firmness of purpose her credibility would immediately be undermined and the entire expedition might well be doomed before it had begun. Consequently she drew on all the emotional reserves at her disposal, gritting her teeth and closing her fists as she curtly snapped: 'Oh, for Heaven's sake, Pobs! It's not your bus! And I'm sure that Eustace will be only too delighted to let you drive at some stage of the journey!'

'I want no favours from the likes of him!' growled Pobs, righting his hat, which had slipped slightly from his head in the course of the struggle. 'He's always had his eyes on Noreen! Pervert!'

'Rest assured you will receive none,' retorted Eustace, acidly.

'Well, all I can say is this is a terrific performance! You two should be proud of yourselves! My daughter over in London – God knows what's happened to her and all you can think of is having ridiculous rows about nothing! Really, Pobs! You ought to be ashamed of yourself!'

If there was a point at which Mrs Tiernan could be said to have made her first mistake, then this was it. For in favouring Eustace in her judgement of the dispute, Mrs Tiernan planted a seed of dissent and resentment which was eventually to grow into an almost impenetrable thicket of raging rebellion and destined to jeopardize the entire operation, not to mention the once-flourishing and mutually cherished relationship between the two men. Sadly, however, she was under the impression that she had dealt admirably with the crisis and was clapping her hands smartly and calling, 'Everybody hurry up now!' as Fr Luke reappeared in the doorway of Spud-U-Like, licking his lips. 'There youse are!' exclaimed the priest good-humouredly as he climbed aboard the minibus. Within minutes they were all set to go, and as they turned out of the village, Fr Luke summed up everybody's feelings as he stuck his upraised thumb out the window and cried: 'Farewell, Barntrosna! Till we see you again – with Noreen Tiernan aboard, looking every bit as fresh and well as the day she left us!'

Which was a trifle optimistic of Fr Luke, and sadly just about as far from the truth as it was possible to get. For not only was Noreen neither fresh nor well-looking, she was just about recognizable and no more. At least as 'Noreen Tiernan'.

Once upon a time – it can hardly be denied – the idea of

Noreen *swearing*, never mind hissing viciously, 'Fork it out, wimp! You pathetic little nothing! Every penny you've got – you hear?' as she held an open razor to the neck of a terrified businessman would have been laughable, and utterly pre- posterous.

But not now. Most definitely, not now. If Mrs Tiernan, as the minibus cruised evenly along the road to Dublin City to make its way to the Holyhead ferry, had possessed the slightest inclination of how her daughter's life had been proceeding of late, she would, quite simply, have had a heart attack on the spot and that would have put paid there and then to the Barntrosna mission of mercy. There would have been no alternative but to turn the vehicle around and return once more to Barntrosna, despondent and Noreenless. Indeed, in retrospect, it might have been as well if this had happened.

It didn't, however, and now onward sped the cheery coachload of close neighbours and clergyman, their minds intent on one thing and one thing alone – to get to the bottom once and for all of what they in their own minds now saw as 'The Noreen Tiernan Mystery'.

Which, of course, was no mystery at all, far from it indeed. Certainly not, at any rate, when she opened the door of the room, finding herself the surprised recipient of a visit from the London Metropolitan Police. From, in particular, a Detective Inspector Dobbs, who claimed to be acting on information received to the effect that she had been connected with the operation of a protection racket in the Brick Lane district of London's East End. There can be no doubting Stephanie's magnificently theatrical performance on that occasion, a stag- geringly seamless blend of innocence and ignorance, aided and abetted by a fast-learning Noreen, who continually interrupted with poignant cries of: 'But we're just nurses! Finishing our first year! How could we possibly be involved with anything like that?' Interspersing these pleas, of course, with heart-rending bursts of weeping. Had it been another policeman, Noreen's protests that she was but another innocent girl from a small town in Ireland who had never been in a big city before would probably have worked. But not with Detective Inspector Dobbs. He had seen too much and been around too long to be fooled by such rustic female wiles. 'No, sweetheart,' he declared, inspecting his spotlessly clean fingernails, 'your girlfriend here's guilty as hell and she knows it. Now you can come along with me quietly or you can make it difficult for yourself. So – which is it going to be?'

In the event, Stephanie cooperated with the police. But not without surreptitiously – expertly – passing a packet to Noreen after a visit to the 'toilet' as she was led away. With trembling hands, Noreen opened it to discover that it contained a white powder, accompanied by a hastily written note which read: *'Noreen – call to the station and use this! You hear? Don't mess it up! See you soon, chicken. Love you!'*

It goes without saying, of course, that the visit of the Metropolitan Police to the private rooms of Noreen and Stephanie had not gone unnoticed, and when she found herself interviewed by both Tank and the deputy head nurse the irritation she felt as a result of their persistent, needle-sharp interrogations combined to ignite in her an emotional combustion which led to a verbal response which truly shocked both Tank and her deputy out of their shoes. As it did Noreen, indeed, for she had never spoken to anyone like that in her life! Not to mention the realization, as it was happening, that she had enjoyed it! 'Oh shut up, you heifer,' she continued, 'what do you know about Stephanie! What Diggsy does is her own business! She doesn't have to answer to anyone else and neither do I! So why don't you take your stupid job and shove it! Shove it where the monkey shoved the nuts, fat arse!'

If there is a point at which the transformation of Noreen Tiernan can be said to have become complete, then this was it. Her swagger as she flung her duffel bag over her shoulder and strode out the gates of the hospital was not that of a student nurse devoted to the care of the elderly and infirm but of a young, unconscionable girl who, as she would often say later, would smoke 'all the drugs' and consume as much 'lifted champagne' as she liked because she didn't 'give a facking toss, mate, and you'd better believe it!'

*

The policeman, as luck would have it, on duty in Paddington Police Station that night was PC Derek Ruddings. Beside him, at his right hand, was a steaming cup of tea. The same tea, as she fixed the befuddled constable with her sensual gaze, thereby distracting his attention, into which Noreen Tiernan now emptied the snow-white contents of her cellophane packet. 'Oh Derek – darling!' she continued as she stroked his cheek with her long green fingernails, proceeding eagerly with this action until the middle-aged man (he and his wife had of late been having problems – she accused him of being 'married to his job' and 'swimming in the sewers' and he suspected her of having an affair with Norman Cousins, a bachelor gardener who lived next door) was eagerly divesting himself of all his clothing.

*

God, how I loathe men now! thought Noreen Tiernan as the policeman panted lasciviously above her, still thinking it as she perceived his eyelids beginning to droop and stroking his curly head softly and soothingly until he was helplessly asleep on top of her. Extricating herself from beneath his seal-like, law-enforcing bulk, she was taken aback to find an image, however fleeting, of Pobs, her 'former' boyfriend as she now considered him, coming into her mind. 'Eurgh! What a pig!' she exclaimed as she retrieved her black patent court shoe from beneath the slumbering custodian's right ear and made her way hurriedly past the filing cabinets out into the wailing cacophony of the night streets.

*

Pobs in the minibus dreaming: of a cottage and a little baby. A little Pobs with Noreen's eyes. For the first time in so long, he felt a twinge of optimism. As the minibus soared down the M1, at last a smile slid across his face. 'It *will* be as we planned it!' he cried aloud. 'We *will* have a lovely little cottage and a baby with Noreen's face and my face and I can work on the farm and Noreen will come home every evening from Barn-trosna General Hospital just like she'd never been away.'

These were the dreams of Pobs McCue, whose heart beat wildly as they sped past Joe's Service Station – making him want to declaim joyfully to the vast stretch of motorway that unrolled itself across the built-up countryside: 'It *has* worked out! I knew it would! I knew my Noreen would never deceive me! Damn and blast all who thought otherwise!'

It was unlike Pobs to swear but on this occasion it could be permitted, considering the fact that for over a year he'd had to endure the sly insinuations of so many of his fellow Barntrosna townspeople. Some of whom made it clear to him in no uncertain fashion that they had their own views as to what was occupying Noreen Tiernan in London and why no communi-cation of any kind appeared to be forthcoming from 'that department' as they coyly termed it. As Parps Henderson, one night in his cups, had bluntly put it: 'She's took up with some fancy man so you may be stirring your tea with your todger from now on, McCue, for Noreen Tiernan's one chancy Angel of Mercy you won't be seeing about the streets of Barntrosna again!'

*

A signpost for Rugby sped past as Pobs chuckled quietly to himself. His shoulders heaved and his teeth chattered. What a lot of stupid-looking fools there were going to be in his hometown when he motored down the main street of Barntrosna with Noreen at his side sporting her glittering engagement ring. When that day came – and by the looks of things it wasn't too far away – they were going to see a very different side of Pobs McCue. For too long he had phlegmatically endured their patronizing comments. How often had he heard them remark 'Ah sure Pobs is grand!' or 'Pobs is not the worst.' Well, when he returned with his bride-to-be at his side they'd soon see what he was made of. Parps Henderson and all the other pass-remarkable doubting Thomases had better look out then!

Let us not forget too that there was another upon that bus who also harboured his private dreams: Fr Luke Doody, who, if he had ever had the courage to admit it, would have shared with anyone who cared to listen the dark secret that he sometimes found life in Barntrosna dull. Not that he considered his parishioners bereft in terms of social skills and capacity for engaging with life. The contrary was true, indeed, for there was not one of them he did not love dearly and would have, like Christ, have died for them if needs be; but the endless round of venial sins, baptisms and predictable

202

liaisons between the boys and girls of the town could often prove wearying, beginning as they did, once again, the cycle of birth and death as it inevitably proceeded. Often, when he was seated by the roaring log fire that Mrs Corg (his house-keeper of many years) would have prepared for him, he would find himself wondering what life might be like in the great city of London for a man like him; to minister in a teeming metropolis where it would be commonplace to have wild-eyed fellows with their insides ravaged by Aids and other similar diseases hammering on your door at midnight begging for forgiveness; to have prostitutes and devil women ringing you up at God knows what time pleading for guidance; to have people losing their religion right left and centre and then wanting it back again; people who did not know what they wanted; men marrying men; drug addicts who would stab all before them just to get more drugs – how exciting it would be to do God's work in such a whirling, white-light vortex! How he envied young Fr Pep, who visited the presbytery each year on his holidays, mesmerizing him with such tales. 'You wouldn't believe it, Father,' he said once, 'only last weekend I had three murderers and an embezzler. I'll tell you, Father, it's non-stop action in St John's Wood.'

The moment he had heard these words uttered, Fr Luke was saddened. He felt deep down inside that his life had become routine, as exciting as a wet dishcloth cast disdainfully onto the tiles of a presbytery floor on some grey November morning. But knew in his heart and soul that putting in for a transfer now would be a simple waste of time. He could just imagine the Bishop's face. 'Would you go away out of that, Fr Luke!' he heard him say, or 'What in under God has got into you these days at all!' pulling out the drawer of his big oaken desk to remove a bottle of C of the B (Cream of the Barley whiskey), and cheerfully exhorting him to 'Have a wee dram there and put that old nonsense out of your head like a good man!'

Fr Luke sighed. He could understand the Bishop's reaction – for that, he knew, and always had, was how everyone perceived him – a true pillar of the Church: solid; unbending before the fickle winds of change; a bollard hammered into the firmest of earth. As the minibus switched lanes, Fr Luke's eyes brightened when he thought of Fr Pep breezily arriving at Barntrosna presbytery, clad from head to toe in his summer 'duds' of bright-coloured shirt (palm trees swaying against a background of purple, he recalled), sandals and loose cotton slacks. He might be old fashioned in his way, the minibus-ferried clergyman now amused himself by thinking, but he had been able to tell by the twinkle in the younger man's eye that he was up to mischief. 'Come on!' Fr Pep had said. 'Come on, Fr Lukey! I have a surprise for you!'

On foot of this reminiscence, before he knew it, Fr Luke found himself – transcendent power of the imagination! – sitting in the passenger seat of an open-topped Alfa Romeo sports car and not in a London-bound minibus at all, heading off down another motorway altogether (LA-bound, perhaps! Or San José even! *Do you by chance know the way?*' he laughed to himself as he thought of him calling to some passing Mexican or Puerto Rican driver!), lush gay strings sweeping out from the car radio as Fr Pep shouted over them: 'What do you think of this little baby, Fr Lukey? Cool, eh?' And, with his greying hair flying out behind him in the silky Californian breeze, the older clergyman being able to make one and only one reply: 'You got it, Fr Pep!'

This was but the stuff of fantasy, however, for the Volks-wagen minibus was no sports car, and their mission had little to do with the attainment of spurious American West Coast baubles such as choice acting parts but with the location of Noreen Tiernan, that and nothing else, apart from her subsequent safe passage home. Neither would there be time, as he now came to realize, and it had been foolish of him to consider otherwise, for meeting Aids victims, or lending an ear to the most unmentionable, possibly unpardonable sins the human mind could ever begin to conceive of, of prostitutes and every other manner of amoral deviant. It saddened Fr Luke. Of course it did. He would have gladly given generously of his time to ladies of the night and the problems of men with donkeys and gas masks. But that was the way it was and there was nothing could be done about it now. Perhaps, he sighed, there would one day come a time when he would be awakened by the sound of red-eyed, possibly deranged maniacs battering feverishly on the door of his presbytery, crying: 'Father! Help me! God, please! Help me, Father! Help me! Help me! Help me!' – but not on this trip.

*

Eustace De Vere-Bingham, his eyes glittering as he sat at the leopardskin-covered steering-wheel, had his dreams too. For the truth was that, many years before, he had been engaged to be married to a young girl who had later left him and who was indeed responsible for his eventual return to the family seat of De Vere-Bingham Hall in Barntrosna. And, side by side with that, there existed an even deeper truth – the fact that Eustace De Vere-Bingham had *no* interest whatsoever in butterflies, and had to be compelled by his brigadier father to direct his attention towards the field of lepidoptera – 'I'll see you do it! You'll be proficient at something, you fool you!' the words echoed. He winced at the reminiscence. For the plain truth was that it would not, in fact, have bothered him in the slightest if local youths had in the dead of night broken into his mansion and put every accursed one of the powder-winged nonentities to the torch. Eustace De Vere-Bingham held no brief for them (no more than he did for his own 'family', many years previously having publicly denounced his father – in fact, all of his forebears – as 'idiots' and 'know-nothing Lilliputian would-be tyrants in tweeds' whilst he set off to 'discover the world' and '*live!*').

As in De Vere-Bingham Hall now, aged far beyond his years, he would pace the floor nightly in a smoking jacket with oriental patterns on it as he raked his fingers through his prematurely greying hair, pausing only to howl 'Alicia!' and stare wild-eyed through the French windows which opened to the south. (But which were rarely open now.)

'Alicia!' he would cry, punching with startling vigour the Restoration-style upholstery of the chaise longue, as he repaired once more to the ever-diminishing drinks cabinet. 'Alicia Taylor de Montfort! God, how I loved you,' he would choke before flicking the switch on his Bell and Howell projector and sobbing softly as the shuddering images of pink-hued girls obliterated the entire back wall with their volleyball-fisting shrieks of delight and cries of 'Eek!' Pursued by rambunctious playboys in the sad, narrative-less tales perennially set in a blank, timeless world of velour push-U-ups and cocktail jazz which seemed the faded aristocrat's only source of pleasure now – including *Sweat-O-Rama Treats* and *Wrassling She-Babes of the 60s*.

Yes, but these were as nothing to the ultimate dream of Eustace De Vere-Bingham – to have his beloved Alicia returned to him. But not for the reasons that might at first be suspected, such as the loving and cherishing of her for the rest of their mortal days together. Which in a normal person might not be an unreasonable supposition. But which was totally and utterly redundant in the case of Eustace De Vere-Bingham. Because the truth was, however unpalatable, that, unbeknownst to anyone – his fondness for 'loops' and 'nudie-grinding' aside – Eustace De Vere-Bingham was, in fact, a deeply disturbed man. If such were not the case, why then did he, on those long nights when he paced the expensively upholstered floors of the family seat and assaulted inanimate objects – stuffed owls, ottomans, eighteenth-century com-modes and the like – inexplicably cry: 'You dare defy me! You dare defy Eustace De Vere-Bingham! Then there is only one thing for it, my dear Alicia! You must die! Do you hear me? Die, I said!' A declaration invariably succeeded by swirl-ing cries which wove their menacing way about the Gothic interior of the mansion like a night-crawling severed hand with fingers of ice. It was no accident that – incongruously, of course, in his Norfolk jacket – the customer most often seen paying visits to Nobby's Videos to peruse such lurid-boxed titles as *Don't Go in the House*, *My Family – Monsters*, *Deranged* and *Stay Away From The Window*! was none other than – Eustace De Vere-Bingham! Who, as perhaps only Nobby the proprietor knew, thought little of packing at least a dozen tapes into a fishing bag before his bubble-shaped conveyance tore off through the village in a cloud of sputtering, smoke and clanking exhaust pipes (one of his failings – despite his intelligence – was the fact that he lacked the patience essential for proper motor vehicle maintenance) before flinging himself with a menacing smirk onto the chaise longue and pressing the 'play' button, thenceforward to cynically graft the visage and other body parts of his former beloved onto the frames of the poor unfortunate females who seemed to have little respite from the misfortune visited upon them by the succession of slavering, dungaree-clad defectives and social misfits who derived particular pleasure from the application of crude workshop tools and other implements to assorted parts of the human anatomy.

It is not with any sense of pleasure that an author reports a grown man – in particular, one of such refinement! – kicking his legs gaily and cheering: 'How do you like that, Alicia! Abandon me now, why don't you, bitch! Ha ha ha! Chop her up! Choppity choppity! Oh boy! Oh yes! The former Mrs De Vere-Bingham! Not quite so forward now, one opines!'

Yes, dear readers – a Barntrosna secret, indeed, for these were the *true* dreams of Eustace De Vere-Bingham; sick, macabre fantasies of blood-revenge, horror and murder of the most grisly kind beside which 'nudie-cuties' were as the most laughable and innocent of fairy tales! A mere red herring cunningly devised by him and willingly – slavishly – credited by the ingenuous, hopelessly good-natured locals.

'No no! Please!' came the helpless teenage cry once more as her bird-boned silhouette appeared upon a background of lurid flock wallpaper as cheap electronic music soared and the rotating bit of the drill moved ever closer.

'Oh but yes!' issued the cry from the lips of Eustace De Vere-Bingham as the deranged, acne-devastated youth ('Alex') leered and closed in remorselessly. 'Oh but yes, you see!'

*

Of all the Barntrosna residents in the minibus that night, beyond question perhaps the most level-headed and realistic of all was Mrs Dolores Tiernan. And of course the reasons why this might be are obvious; after all, it was *her* daughter's plight which had precipitated the mission of mercy in the first place.

She could not afford to squander valuable time construing herself as some hotshot middle-aged detective from a small Irish village who was destined to astound the London Metropolitan Police with dry wit and pointlessly contrived idiosyncrasies. But there were occasional instances – and it would be dishonest to state otherwise – when the notion did not appear entirely unattractive and she would permit herself a wry, private smile. Seeing, perhaps, her small round form encased in a belted fawn mackintosh, a snub-nose revolver snug deep inside her pocket as she 'laid it on the line'.

That was the only way to get results, she heard herself say. Hit 'em hard and hit 'em fast. That way they had respect for you. 'Don't you jerk with me!' She sighed as the words came to her, her reverie evaporating now, for the idea of her cursing at anyone – never mind a policeman! – was just about the last thing you could ever imagine Dolores Tiernan doing. It wasn't the kind of situation she found herself in.

But this wasn't just any situation, and she knew it. Her daughter was missing and if extreme measures were called for, she would not be found wanting! 'I want you to find my daughter and I want you to find her now! You got that?' she would bark – and without a moment's hesitation – if she felt it necessary. And they would have got it, all right, as she flung her cigar stump into the wastepaper basket and stormed out through the frosted glass door, disgusted.

*

But not half as disgusted as the policeman who had been guarding Stephanie was when he woke up with a mechanical digger churning up the inside of his skull and the cell door wide open. He stumbled blindly out the door of the station. Outside the red buses heaved and the black cabs throbbed in the slipstream. He sank his closed fist into his palm and cursed violently again. But it was to no avail, for of Stephanie Diggs and Noreen Tiernan there was no sign to be seen.

*

Unless you counted a sighting some nights later in the small hours of Saturday morning when a young man who had been out on the town celebrating his birthday looked up instinctively and through the fog that enveloped him (a consequence of eighteen bottles of Tuborg ale) experienced what can only be called the shock of his life – for there, leaning up against the damp brick of a seedy Soho sidestreet was a girl, her body completely, from head to foot, encased in black leather, smiling suggestively at him as a long cigarette dangled from her lips. 'Got a light, darling?' she enquired huskily. In his enthusiasm (he was already frantically searching his pockets) and disorientation, the unfortunate youth did not see the other figure emerge from the shadows; nor discern the starlike gleam of the open razor before it was coldly pressed to the flesh of his neck. 'Give us your money! All of it!' snapped Stephanie Diggs as she cast the remainder of her cigarette to the ground, whereupon it died with a hiss in a shining puddle. Noreen breathlessly fingered the notes stuffed into his wallet. 'And if you ever breathe a word of this, we'll come looking for you!' she hissed, in an accent in every way almost identical to Stephanie's.

'Yes! Please – please don't kill me!' the pathetic youth now pleaded.

'Next time that's exactly what we'll do!' snapped Noreen as she pushed him forward gruffly. 'Now get out of here if you know what's good for you! Before we do something really naughty!'

'Like cut your nibblies off!' barked Stephanie after him, before hurling herself onto what can only be termed a roller coaster of heartlessly mocking laughter.

Which echoed shrilly through the night-time streets of the city of London as at last (their night's work done) they made their way home to the East End apartment where they now lived on their ill-gotten gains and proceeds of their crimes. Nothing fazed them any longer – trepidations, such as they had been, now a thing of the past – as was plainly evident the moment they opened the door and entered the flat, Noreen shrieking with renewed vigour as she kicked off her stilettos and fell upon the bed (peach satin sheets!) crying: 'Oh, Diggsy! Did you see his face! His poor little face!' while Stephanie lit a cigarette and poured them both a drink, replying wickedly: 'Sure did, chicken!'

There followed a period of relative silence as they turned over the events of the evening in their minds, sipping delight-edly as further plans for the future unfolded – almost telepath-ically – in their minds.

About that night but one thing is certain: the girl lying on the bed with one leg folded and the white flesh of thigh gleaming with startling clarity above the top of her liquorice-black hose who had once been the most dutiful and responsible girl in all of Barntrosna village was no longer that girl. And, with each day that passed, behind the trowel-loads of eye shadow and knife-slashes of fire engine red lipstick, the mem-ory of what had once been Noreen Tiernan, holy Barntrosna girl, student nurse, was fading fast and would soon clearly vanish from the face of the earth as surely as if it had never existed.

*

To say that the sister superior was taken aback when she looked up from her desk at which she was occupied filling in the timetable for the girls in the throat cancer ward would be an understatement, indeed as the smoggy, stuttering minibus trailed to a halt outside the hospital building what actually happened was that her spectacles fell off and she sat there for some moments with her pen poised upright at a ninety-degree angle as she did her level best to make sense of the drama which was now – somewhat haphazardly – unfolding on the forecourt directly outside the window. Eustace De Vere-Bingham, patting the lapels of his Norfolk jacket, was calmly surveying the immaculately landscaped terrain as if it belonged entirely to him.

Of the little gathering which was now assembled beneath the plaque which read St Bartholomew's General Hospital, Opened by HM The Queen, March 13 1959, perhaps the least imposing was Pobs McCue and this was directly related to the unfathomable depth of shyness within him which had begun many years before in Barntrosna Primary School when his then teacher – Master Gunn – had dragged him out before the class and cuffed him gruffly on the back of the head, snarling pitilessly as his nine-year-old charges (forty of them) chuckled with a mixture of amusement and terror.

'Well, good man McCue!' he barked. 'I suppose you're going to make an ass of yourself again in the County Scholarship this year!'

Ever since that day, whenever he found himself confronted by figures of authority, Pobs would perceive himself to be as worthless and of as little import as some inconsequential piece of mud you would find in the middle of Barntrosna main street on the rainiest day of the season.

Thoughts which were now coursing through his head as he

fiddled with his fingers and, through hooded, horsehair-rimmed eyes, looked up to see the hazy figure of the sister superior (Tank, of course!) now rising from her desk. Last to emerge from the minibus was Fr Luke, who, without warning, took it upon himself to begin something of a lengthy intellectual discourse with a bewildered Pobs as regards the cultural differences between Ireland and England and the procession of sub-textual disapprovals their little party might expect in the course of forthcoming dialogues.

In all her long career the sister superior had never been confronted by such an eclectic grouping. She was quite at a loss for words. But when she heard them declare what the purpose of their visit actually was, she became utterly speechless. A glazy film appeared over her eyes and in a dry, hoarse voice, she addressed herself exclusively to Mrs Tiernan, whom she instinctively – and quite correctly, as it happened – assumed to be the spokesperson.

Fr Luke found himself saddened by the nurse's lack of compassion. It was misunderstandings such as these that led to wars and hatred between peoples, he reflected. Eustace De Vere-Bingham, however, assumed no such attitude. He stiffened with outrage as the nurse suddenly – unforgivably – snapped at Mrs Tiernan: 'Yes! She turned out to be quite a little madam, didn't she – your little daughter! Coming here with the sweet Miss Colleen Irish act – butter wouldn't melt in her mouth – and the next thing you know she's involved not only in lesbian affairs but waylaying unsuspecting people right, left and centre! No, nursing wasn't good enough for her! Or that half-man, half-woman trollop she took up with! Couldn't be satisfied with an honest day's work for an honest day's pay, could she, no, it had to be mugging if you don't mind, razor gangs, drugs and God knows what else!'

By the time she was finished, it was all Pobs could do not to remove his large bunched fist from the inside of his pocket and put her through the plate-glass window. Astute as he was, and possessing a deep, instinctive knowledge of the vagaries of his parishioners, Fr Luke laid a steadying hand on his shoulder, followed by a cautionary, firm knitting of the brow and the soft whisper: 'Easy now, Pobs.'

'This is an outrage! An outrage and nothing less!' snapped Eustace De Vere-Bingham suddenly as Mrs Tiernan, close now to tears, summoned all the reserves of courage and dignity she had at her disposal and, chokingly, replied: 'One day you'll pay for what you've said to me here, Nurse. One day you will pay for those bitter uncompromising words! My Noreen might not be a saint but it's a disturbed and twisted woman who would make up lies the like of that! Maybe we're not swanky nurses or fancy doctors or government ministers! Maybe we *are* from stupid old Barntrosna. But we're still human beings! And I know that when my Noreen left our house she was as happy as the day is long and nothing – nothing! – would have pleased her more than to help old people or read stories to children whose situations are hopeless! And now here you are telling me that's not true? Where is my Noreen? What have you done with her?' The tears were pouring from Mrs Tiernan's eyes now and her voice had shrunk to the size of a marrowfat pea. But this ought not to be taken as an indication that her fury had in any way diminished – for it most certainly had not!

If you had informed anyone back in Barntrosna of what transpired next, employing perhaps the words: 'Can you believe it – Mrs Tiernan hitting the sister superior a box?' you simply wouldn't have been given any credence. As indeed, why ought you, for up until this moment Mrs Tiernan had never hurt anyone in her life, never mind sisters superior and people in authority. Indeed, nobody was more surprised than the fifty-year-old woman herself when she slowly raised her small, weather-beaten fist and planted it fair and square in the middle of the hirsute nurse's jaw. The nurse who now, whitefaced, fell back onto a pile of gravel directly behind her with her skirt billowing up around her waist in the manner of a landed parachutist. A trembling Mrs Dolores Tiernan stood over her, tentatively rubbing her bruised knuckles. Pobs McCue leaped forward, his eyes on fire. 'It's what you deserve, you heartless thug!' he tremulously cried, placing a protective arm around the shoulders of his courageous long-time neighbour.

Eustace De Vere-Bingham, intoxicated by the vehemence of Mrs Tiernan's response, was then astonished to find himself leaping forward and standing over the perplexed hospital employee, crying: 'Ha, ha! Die! Yeah – you heard me! You got that, whore? Ha ha! Hee hee! Ha ha!'

As he often reflected – fearfully, indeed – for many years after, while hypnotized by the beguiling light of the cathode-ray tube, it was the mercy of God that he did not, at that moment, have a machete or screwdriver or ordinary garden tool at his disposal. (The hurt Alicia – and, by extension, the entire race of females – had caused him was still a vibrant, living thing.)

Even Fr Luke found it difficult to restrain himself. But, undoubtedly, the greatest effect was that which it had on Pobs, who now raced forward and hit the stumbling nurse an almighty kick in the flank, crying belligerently, 'That's for Noreen!' as he retreated, stunned, as though some powerful unnamed drug had, out of nowhere, somehow managed to shoot itself directly into his bloodstream.

*

If perhaps they had experienced any success whatsoever in locating Noreen in the early stages of their campaign the psychological adhesive which bound the earnest investigative team together might never have begun to soften and ultimately melt away as it did. They did not, however. And in the to them alien city of London, this was ultimately to prove fatal. For, adrift from the emotional moorings which had inextricably bound them to the beloved town and hinterland of Barntrosna, it was not long before a deep uncertainty began to manifest itself within each individual. And which, as it inevitably must, led to the fractious, confrontational behaviour which became such a feature of the investigative party in the latter days. Perhaps if Fr Luke had not – quite by chance – been approached by an emaciated youth who clutched feverishly at his arm and begged him to hear his confession, the cracks might not have begun to appear – at least with such alacrity – and they could have continued to function for somewhat longer as a happy unit. But appear they did and when Fr Luke, after admittedly quite a tortuous wrestling match with his conscience, announced one night whilst they were all consuming cans of Pepsi around a tar-smelling bonfire that he now considered his duties lay elsewhere, the die was cast. As Pobs realized, his can suspended before his chalk-coloured face, it was truly the beginning of the end.

The old priest looked sadly at the pale farmer, and lowering his head as if it was an unbearable weight, softly, to the question, 'Does this mean what I think it means?' provided the answer: 'I'm afraid it does, Pobs.'

Now Pobs McCue had never sworn at a priest before in his life but this was clearly more than he could bear. 'You mean to tell me,' he began chokingly, 'that we have come all this way to look for Noreen and now you're just going to

216

race off with some fly-by-night drug addicts you met on the street?'

This choice of words incensed the priest. 'They are *not* drug addicts!' he snapped indignantly.

'Well, go on, then!' retorted Pobs. 'Go on! For if that's the way you feel about it we don't need your help anyway!'

Perhaps if they had called him back as he wound his way into the black, smoky London night, he might indeed have returned. Who knows? And who can say that it was not meant to be that way and that after a lifetime of venial sins and hopelessly innocent escapades that could hardly be called sins at all he now had tales told to him in confession about murders and robberies and rapes and what have you, subjects of which heretofore he could only longingly dream.

One thing was certain – as far as the minibus shuttle of nocturnal investigations was concerned, irreparable damage had been done. Now Mrs Tiernan, overwrought by emotion, was prone to bursting without warning into tears – something which would have been utterly unthinkable before. No matter where they went in London, they began to perceive people laughing at them. 'What? See her? In a city of ten million people? You've just got to be out of your mind, mate! Bladdy 'ell! Takes all kinds, don't it? Farking missing nurses!'

Such seemed – indeed *were* – the responses of myriad petrol-pump attendants and saloon bar keepers.

*

Poor Pobs was heartbroken. He had begun to fear now that he would never see his loved one again. As he declared hoarsely one night, having consumed enormous quantities of ale, 'She could be dead! Murdered! Dumped in a godforsaken bin somewhere!'

Which, of course, she wasn't, because right at that very moment she was climbing into a brand-new pair of leather trousers (stolen, of course!), and preparing herself for yet another profitable night on the town, as her soul mate and partner in crime adjusted a brass nose ring and winked at her from the triptych mirror, smiling as she said: 'You all right, then, Noreen Pussycat?'

Yes, Noreen Tiernan was all right. No doubt about it! Would that the same could have been said for her mother, who was as far now from a discerning, capable investigator as it was possible to get, perilously close indeed to what might be described as a crushed and broken remnant of an Irish country housewife. After the others had taken their leave of her and vanished somewhere into the bowels of the pulsing city, she would remain alone in the minibus, thinking back on fields full of buttercups through which Noreen would come running towards her in a lovely little print dress, ecstatically crying: 'Mammy! Mammy! Mammy!' Her body would shudder then as she sat there thinking of how stupid she had been to come over near this cold and heartless place! How could she ever have believed she would find her daughter in this vertiginous landscape of kaleidoscopic madness? How could she – a poor, simple, round-shaped, unassuming woman – ever have hoped to triumph in an alien culture? People did not listen to small curly-haired women in plain, unassuming clothes and furry boots, most of all, consider them – how could they? – detectives. No doubt, had she been a burly, uncompromising man with a half-eaten hamburger or a polystyrene cup things would have been different, had she hurled files and snapped into handsets, threatening to go 'right up to City Hall!' if nothing was done. But Mrs Tiernan couldn't do that. She didn't even know where City Hall was. No, she now knew (and the realization stung her – she would never make a detective. She would never be anything more than a poor stupid worthless – and now daughter-less – lump of a housewife stuck in the cab of a minibus in a nightscape of no names and broken dreams.

Or so she thought. And indeed might have been absolutely right and gone on being just that if Pobs McCue, in the Piccadilly area of the city, had not found his way into a certain late-night dancing club (Madame Pork's!) – a truly extraordinary achievement considering the amount of Tuborg he had consumed over the course of the day – and there encountered one Augustus 'Gus' Halpin, celebrated manager of the Barntrosna branch of the First National Bank, emerging from a velvet-draped cubicle, not in his customary sober grey suit, but in a bias-cut burgundy gown that reached right down to his knees! Not only that, but clutching a tortoiseshell cigarette-holder!

'Gus!' gasped Pobs in astonishment as he fell back against the wall.

*

What exactly was happening inside the body of Pobs McCue as he slow-danced now beneath the rotating mirrorball, placing his large freckled hand on the shoulder of the transformed bank manager who was now smiling wryly – and not a little hungrily!? Something which he, for certain, had never before experienced. It was as if every red corpuscle in his bloodstream had received a klaxonlike command to make at once for the immediate vicinity of his cheeks, followed by reinforcements whose responsibility it was to serve the area in the upper back and neck region. With the result that when the smiling, lip-glossed and seriously heavily made-up employee of the Barntrosna branch of the First National Bank turned to flicker her eyelids and coo 'sweet nothings', what met her gaze was not a handsome, copper-haired youth but a livid, scarlet-complexioned man in his late twenties who appeared to be on the verge of a nervous breakdown and a heart attack at the same time. And, perhaps in a small way, it did indeed disappoint her. For he was no Tom Cruise, that is for certain, and what girl, politically committed feminist or otherwise, does not harbour a secret desire to be spirited away to the murky fastness of some dark Prince Charming, there to be seriously tackled until the dawn breaks? But there are too other important things in life – things such as love, for example. For how long can such unbridled physical ravaging continue before beginning to pale? Which was why Augusta pushed back the tumbling copper curls, and throwing caution to the winds, flung her arms around his neck and sank her tongue deep into the unsuspecting Pobs McCue's mouth.

*

The concept of 'clubbing' was one quite unknown to Pobs McCue, and when Augusta gripped him by the arm and cried excitedly, 'I know what we'll do, Pobs, darling! We'll go to the Ring of Feathers Club! What do you say?' he simply hadn't the faintest idea how to respond. And compliantly followed her lead as she cooed: 'Ooh! What a good idea!' chuckling tipsily as they fell out into the night, the bank manager hoisting her skirts as she inserted two fingers in between her pink lips and whistled shrilly for a cab.

What fun they had on the way over! Augusta just could not get over the sheer coincidence of meeting – in London, a city of ten million people, for heaven's sake! 'Oh now!' Pobs repeated – a little nervous still, it has to be admitted, as the bank manager kept squeezing his leg and fluttering her eyelashes at him, 'sure you wouldn't think it would happen in a million years!'

Any more than you would think what happened next would be within the remotest bounds of possibility. Somehow, between the cab and the Ring of Feathers (which was only a matter of twenty yards away), they managed to become separated and just at the point when Augusta was about to call, 'Wait for me!' she found herself roughly grabbed from behind and the cold steel of an open razor glinting from the shadows pressed coldly to her neck. 'Take that!' cried Stephanie Diggs as she laid the flat of her hand on Augusta's cheek. 'See how you like that, honey!'

The former nurse stood back as the bank manager's blonde wig fell into the gutter.

'Help me! Help me, Pobs!' squealed Augusta, cradling his heavily made up face in his hands.

'Oh no! Oh my God! Noreen!' cried Pobs as the blood began to drain from his cheeks, the woman he loved so much standing staring at him for the first time in what had seemed to him a century!

'Who's this? Huh?' demanded Stephanie Diggs as she manhandled him disdainfully. 'You hear me? Who is this? What's your name? You deaf?'

There are some things you simply cannot explain. Actions of men for which no rationale can ever be found. What followed next is such an action. That Pobs's countenance should pale to the shade of the whitest of flours is to be expected. That he should tremble and stand aghast, also. But that he would suddenly bellow, 'Don't fucking push me! Don't you fucking push me, Hatchet-Face! I'm Pobs! Pobs McCue! And I'm not going to take it any more!' square his fist and hit Stephanie so forcefully on the chin that she collapsed in a dead faint on the street beside him simply could not have been foreseen.

Or indeed what transpired next: Noreen bursting into tears, casting the razor from her as if somehow in that instant she had suddenly been awakened from some black induced hypnosis to cry out, 'Pobs! Oh Pobs!' peppering his red, meaty face with innumerable kisses, as she wept: 'Oh, Pobs! How I've missed you! Darling, how I've missed you!' her eyes lighting up once more as Pobs and Augusta gave her a little wave of solidarity and she found herself crying: 'It's you! Pobs! You're all here! All my old friends! The old Barntrosna friends I should never have left!'

*

Can you even begin to imagine the exultation which swept through Noreen's mother's being when she looked up and through bruised and red-rimmed eyes perceived the sight that was before her? 'It's happened,' she repeated wearily, 'I've finally lost my mind!' It was as if she had indeed done so and been magically spirited away to some glorious Elysian fields where everything would now be as her heart desired it. Except perhaps, without Eustace De Vere-Bingham, who, having spent the entire night in the video shops and basement striptease parlours, had, it would appear, indeed crossed a 'line' of some kind, bringing him as far from the Elysian fields as could possibly be imagined. For now he writhed, trouserless, in the back of the minibus, tweaking his private parts and repeating foolishly: 'So you thought I was gonna give you a ride to Sausalito, did you baby? Seems to me like you went and made a big mistake then, honey! A big mistake, Alicia baby! Ha ha! Ha ha! Hee!' with tears of hopeless laughter rolling down his face.

Mrs Tiernan could not contain herself as she flung open the door of the minibus and went racing towards her first-born.

'Mammy!' cried Noreen as the two women embraced. Continuing, indeed, until they eventually fell over and landed by the side of the road, just narrowly missing a pile of old fruit abandoned by a wheelie bin that would surely have destroyed their clothes.

'Look at us!' exclaimed Mrs Tiernan. 'What's anyone going to think of us, Noreen!'

'Oh now Mammy!' giggled her daughter as Pobs began to clap while Augusta cried excitedly: 'Three cheers for the Tiernans! For no one deserves it more! Hip hip hooray!'

*

On the day that Pobs and Noreen were wed, everyone attended and it turned out to be one of the nicest weddings the town had seen in many a long day. Fr Cyril (the new priest) made a great speech. 'Not too long,' as everyone agreed, 'and not too short.' There was great fun too when the streamer-draped car drove through the streets of Barntrosna with cans tied on and shaving foam jokes written all over the bonnet and the boot. '*Here is the weather forecast – warm and close now – a little son later – ha ha!*' read one of them – and did Pobs's face go red when he saw that!

But that didn't matter any more. For, as far as Pobs was concerned, it could go as red as it liked. It could flush away to beat the band, for now he once more possessed the woman he loved. The woman who, for so long, had been lost to him. As he, indeed, had been lost to her.

And now as the Morris Minor, in its fluttering array of pink and blue, left the main street of the village Noreen

Tiernan wondered how she could ever have done what she did. How could she have left the man she had loved, his heart broken in who knew how many places? Left him there to pine for her in dreary, dismal solitude. All of a sudden, she felt dreadful. 'You're a hallion, Noreen Tiernan!' she chided herself silently behind the lace curtain of her veil. 'A hallion and a haverel to go and do the like of that! How could you do it?'

But to those questions she had no answers. The only answer came in the form of an ethereal image that drifted almost imperceptibly past the frontiers of her consciousness. That of a leather-clad, nose-ringed she-devil who – *even yet!* – persisted – from a penumbral abyss within her – with her seductive exhortations! Exhortations to 'Leave him! Leave the stupid fool! Noreen! Come back to Stef!'

'No!' shrieked Noreen suddenly, startling Pobs as he spun the wheel and cried: 'Jesus Mary and Joseph, Noreen, don't do that! You nearly gave me a heart attack there!'

'I'm sorry,' she apologized softly and touched him gently on the freckled forearm. A moistness began to sparkle in his eyes as Noreen moved closer to him and rested her head on his shoulder.

'No!' came the silent whisper to her mind. 'I will not go back! To you or any of your sick, filthy habits! For that's what you are – sick, Diggsy – sick! Sick! You hear me?'

A detective or psychologist specializing in the field of human behaviour with particular regard to deviance might have noted that she referred to her former companion as 'Diggsy' in this instance and not as 'Stephanie Diggs' or 'Bitch!' or 'Tramp!' or any of the other pejorative appellations she might have been expected to employ. And why might this be? Because – and here is the awful truth! – despite her bitter protestations to the contrary, some clandestine part of Noreen

Tiernan still longed for the life which she now so openly disavowed!

An unquenchable yearning which would only become apparent when, late at night, in the throes of their lovemaking, the face of her husband would slowly, beguilingly transmogrify until it became that of – *Stephanie Diggs!!!!!*, and once again to her ears would come the words which thrilled her so she could barely breathe!

'Like that, do you, chicken? Like it, huh? Don't worry, my little Irish colleen! For there's plenty more where that came from! Take this! And this! Ha ha ha!'

*

Of course, it was never to be known in the town of Barntrosna that Noreen had been involved in torrid lesbian affairs, extortion rackets or razor gangs.

No, about the former activities of Noreen Tiernan there now was drawn a veil of deepest secrecy, and whenever questions were asked, innocently – regarding Noreen's seemingly abrupt abandonment of her burgeoning career – Noreen's mother would always reply: 'Ah sure, that London! It's far too big, I'm telling you! Isn't she as well off out of it!'

Thus the fabric of small-town life remained satisfactorily ravelled, and the good people of Barntrosna permitted to continue with their quiet, untroubled lives. And, years later, when Noreen had little children of her own, all running about playing marbles and football and chasing, no one would ever be able to say: 'There's Noreen's children! Just let us pray they never find the big stack of sado-masochistic lesby magazines under the bed, that's all I can say!'

No – those words would never be able to pass their lips, for of magazines or anything else they would know nothing. All they would know of Noreen McCue was that every day at three o'clock she did her shopping, bought her *Woman's Own* in Tony's newsagents, along with some sweets for the 'little terrors!', and then made her way home to cook Pobs's dinner. Dressed not in leather or chains, but in a lovely little floral pinafore and a sober pair of furry boots, exactly like her mother's. As far as lesbian affairs or razor gangs or extortion rackets were concerned, they might just as well never have existed. They were the stuff of cheap throwaway pulp novels, belonging in the dusty back rooms of sordid would-be libraries in forgotten back streets, and just about as far from the McCue cottage as it was humanly possible to get.

It was sad, of course, when Mrs Tiernan died some weeks after the wedding, but, as Noreen remarked to Pobs: 'At least she died happy, Pobs.' Which indeed she did. Initially, of course, it had been a great shock to her to discover the truth about Noreen but gradually she began to understand. 'As long as you and Pobs do the decent thing and get married, that's all I care about,' she had said, 'and as far as Barntrosna is concerned, if we breathe not a word, nobody will be any the wiser!'

And so Mrs Tiernan went to her grave. As did Augustus Halpin, who very late one night fell down the well upon which he had been standing whilst in full Scarlett O'Hara flow, serenading sheep with a variety of plaintive southern ejaculations. 'How many times did poor old Mr Halpin stand up on that wall and not fall down it?' Parps Henderson remarked in the Bridge on the day that they buried him. 'It's a tragedy! A bloody tragedy! There's no other word for it!'

And there were very few gathered in the afternoon gloom of the Bridge Bar who could disagree with that. Just continuing to sit there shaking their heads and staring at the dazzling array of bottled drinks available behind the counter. 'All the same,' ventured Timmy Cronin after a long pause, 'he was never the same since he went to London. I remarked a great change in him ever since he came back from that place. And I don't just mean the bonnets and dresses and that. I mean generally.'

'Aye,' agreed the Sketch O'Halloran, 'London made him go quare.'

Which, had they but known it, proved equally true of their former pastor, the man for so long they had known as Fr Luke – now, of course, replaced by Fr Cyril – who was never again seen in the town. Never seen because he was too busy saying to heroin and cocaine addicts, 'You've got to trust me!' and giving them bits of furniture and five-pound notes in between falling to his knees and thanking God for giving him 'a second chance'!

Not that it mattered – his being seen or not – for had he walked down the main street they would not have recognized him anyway, attired as he was now in a Peter Wyngarde-style cream safari jacket, scallop-collared peach satin shirt and loose polka-dot cravat.

Of which there was no question in any case – his returning – for he knew there was no point. 'They just wouldn't understand me!' he said to Sick Fellow (not his real name), one of his favourite addicts, as he handed him the twenty-pound note he had promised to give him for methadone some days before.

Eustace De Vere-Bingham too had apparently vanished and all that anyone knew of him they gleaned from the muffled grunts and occasional cackles that emanated from the grim overgrown fastness that was De Vere-Bingham Hall, mingling with the shrieks of semi-clad women being pursued through forests and desolate urban landscapes as cheap electronic music and the multicoloured lights from the cathode-ray tube swirled relentlessly out into the night. To this day, it is not clear whether or not his cherry-red bubble car will ever be seen again about the streets of Barntrosna or the cries of 'There goes the effing Protestant!' echo as in days of yore.

What is clear, however, is that all those who made that fateful journey from the little town of Barntrosna to the city that never sleeps were never, in one way or another, quite the same again. Perhaps the quiet metamorphosis of the psyche which each separate individual had undergone in the course of those anxious, traumatic days is best represented by the high-pitched, nocturnal utterances heard by Pobs McCue as he ran his large bucket-sized hands furiously up and down his wife's back, quite reasonably expecting delirious affirmations of her innermost feelings for him, and instead finding coming to his ears, the words: 'Oh Diggsy! Oh Jesus! Diggsy darling! Give it to me, Steffy baby! Fark me bendy, you mental cah!' a little tear finding its way into his eye as he turned from the woman he loved so much and cried out: 'Oh God! Oh God! Oh God please no!' furiously pounding the pillow until he became exhausted, collapsing hopelessly at last in a Brobdignagian mass of what can only be described as pulverizingly freckled despair.

Phildy Hackball: A Biography

Phildy Hackball has lived in Castleblayney, Newtownforbes, Threemile-
house and Newbliss. In 1972, he left Longford and lived in Nobber,
County Louth. During 1978–79, he settled in Barntrosna, where he
first began to write seriously. His work has been published in antholo-
gies in Cavan, Monaghan and Mullingar, and in 1980, his first short
story ('Cavan Freaks of 1966' – not included here) was published by
Buck-Cat, a radical press based in Carrickmacross. *Mondo Desperado*
is his first book. His major interests are 'the pictures', 'having a few jars'
and 'relaxing with friends'.

Mr Hackball currently lives in Barntrosna, where he is working on a
novel ('with plenty of shooting – and a shark!'), and divides his time
between the Bridge Bar and his home in Main Street.